# KNIGHT

## OF

# Grand Crossing

*Book 5 of the Knights of the Castle Series*

*Hiram Shogun Harris,*
*Anita L. Roseboro, and Naleighna Kai*

Macro Publishing Group
Chicago, Illinois

Knight of Grand Crossing by Hiram Harris, Naleighna Kai, Anita L. Roseboro Copyright ©2020
ISBN: [Ebook] 9781952871030
ISBN: [Trade Paperback] 978-1-952871-11-5

Macro Publishing Group
1507 E. 53rd Street, #858
Chicago, IL 60615

Cover Designed by: J.L Woodson: www.woodsoncreativestudio.com
Interior Designed by: Lissa Woodson: www.naleighnakai.com
Editors: J. L. Campbell jlcampbellwrites@gmail.com; Lissa Woodson
Betas: Debra J. Mitchell, Stephanie M. Freeman, and Kelsie Maxwell

# KNIGHT

## OF

# Grand Crossing

*Book 5 of the Knights of the Castle Series*

*Hiram "Shogun" Harris,*

*Anita L. Roseboro, and*
*Naleighna Kai*

# ♦ DEDICATION ♦

*Hiram "Shogun" Harris*

*I would like to dedicate this book to my mother Cecelia Patrice Fosten, grandmother, Mabel Ann Fosten, and to Renee Sesvalah Cobb-Dishman*

*Naleighna Kai*

*I dedicated this book to Jean Woodson, Eric Harold Spears, LaKecia Janise Woodson, Mildred E. Williams, Anthony Johnson, L. A. Banks, Octavia Butler, Tanishia Pearson Jones, Emmanuel Donnell McDavid, and Priscilla Jackson*

*Anita L. Roseboro*

*Dedicated to my boys, never give up on your dreams.*

# ♦ ACKNOWLEDGEMENTS ♦

Special thanks goes out to the creator: my mother, Cecelia P. Harris, Sesvalah, J. L. Woodson (that cover, though), Debra J. Mitchell, J. L. Campbell, Karen D. Bradley, Unique Hiram, Siera London, Kelsie Maxwell, the members of NK Tribe Called Success, the members of Namakir Tribe, my martial arts crew, my tattoo clients, 9 Mag, Black Ink Chicago . . . thank you all for your support.

*Hiram "Shogun" Harris*

First and foremost, I give thanks to the Creator, for the gifts He has given me. I thank Naleighna Kai for the opportunity to be a part of this project with Hiram Shogun Harris. You are a true mentor and friend. Your encouragement is never failing. Thank you London St. Charles for answering my questions. To J. L. Campbell, Debra Mitchell, Kelsie Maxwell, Stephanie M. Freeman, thank you all for your time and assistance. All of your input was invaluable. Tribe, you are the best group of Authors ever!

*Anita L. Roseboro*

Special thanks goes out to: Sesvalah, J. L. Woodson (for the awesome cover designs for the Knights of the Castle and the Kings of the Castle series), Debra J. Mitchell, J. L. Campbell, Karen D. Bradley, Stephanie M. Freeman, Kelly Peterson, Janine Ingram, Ehryck F. Gilmore, LaVerne Thomspon, Kassanna Dwight, Stephanie M. Freeman, Sandy S., April Bubb, Unique Hiram, Siera London, Kelsie Maxwell, the Kings of the Castle Ambassadors, Members of Naleighna Kai's Literary Cafe, the members of NK Tribe Called Success, the members of Namakir Tribe, and to you, my dear readers . . . thank you all for your support.

Much love, peace, and joy,

*Naleighna Kai*

*Chapter 1*

Ahmad sensed the heat of Susan's gaze on him and knew a heated argument would follow.

"Why are you inviting her to your place?" She demanded, gripping his arm. "She's a total stranger."

He removed his arm from her hold. "A stranger who has more patience with my son than you've ever had," he said, moving toward the wooden bench where Taj was perched next to a woman with dark hair styled in an asymmetrical bob. She had a warm, inviting smile and a passionate nature that enticed him more than Susan Abbott ever could.

Susan flinched and took a step back. "What's that supposed to mean? We get along fine."

"Do you?" he shot back. "Mostly, I see that Taj doesn't want to be around you. Why do you think I made sure to limit your contact with him since he arrived?"

Ahmad watched as Susan's gaze skimmed past the woman who she felt was the current source of contention. This was second to the sudden appearance of his ex-wife, Lauren and his son. Both of whom had traveled from America to Durabia for the medical symposium where Ahmad was listed as a major sponsor and featured presenter.

This brief excursion to Vihaan Park, surrounded by the beach, soccer park, and a children's playground, was a welcome respite from all the seminars, workshops, and facility tours to be held over the next few days.

She trailed him, nearly invading his personal space as she said, "That woman doesn't belong here."

"Oh, so we're back to that, huh?" he asked, putting some distance between them. "No discussion about what I just mentioned concerning your uncomfortable relationship with Taj."

She dismissed him with a wave of her red manicured hand. "Doesn't deserve dignifying with an answer. That woman is simply playing coy to get your attention. And now she has it."

"What is it to you? Why are you so invested in my personal affairs? I keep telling you, we will simply be business associates. Nothing more." Ahmad smirked, finding it humorous that she was quick to point out someone else's flaws but couldn't see her own.

The crestfallen expression on her face wasn't hard to miss. "I only want you to see her for who she really is."

His gaze flickered to the beautiful, voluptuous woman sitting next to his son. Minutes ago, she explained that the tears he had seen her shed weren't the result of being unhappy. She was in the park today writing a scene in a novel, and it touched her so much that tears were the only way to express her feelings.

Taj left Ahmad's side and asked her why the words meant so much. The woman, Alyssa, then took time away from something so important to her to show him how stringing words together expressed thoughts, feelings, and could take the reader on a journey.

Then she had handed his son her tablet and guided him in creating a story of his own, telling him that when an author penned a book, each word, each sentence, each paragraph, each page, each chapter was a code to their thoughts, feelings, and life experiences. The reader had to decipher those letters and phrases. Everyone would find something different based on their own lives and personal experiences. Those things were the lens by which they viewed and interpreted everything in their world. Powerful. Simple. Amazing. His son was almost sitting in the woman's lap, and Ahmad sensed the sincerity of her actions and the incredible connection she had with her art.

Ahmad had taken his son to many specialists over the past few years. This brief interlude with a total stranger had done more for his child than any of those sessions. Taj was a whiz with math and science, but struggled with the written word. In less than two minutes, this woman had broken through that barrier, and his son was writing—actually writing a story from his imagination. So, Ahmad didn't care how Susan, a medical professional who had recently shown up in Durabia, felt about the situation. This unexpected experience was the best thing to happen in his life for a while.

Then he remembered what Susan had said. *I only want you to see her for who she really is.*

"And who is that, exactly?" he tossed back.

"An opportunist," Susan countered, as though he should have figured that out for himself. "She's not even on the same level as we are."

"She's a creative," Ahmad replied so only she could hear, taking in the smile his son bestowed on Alyssa. "We all embrace creative energy. I admire her gift because I'm a creative myself." He maneuvered to one side so a family of American tourists could move around them. "And there are no such thing as levels. Are you suggesting that you are somehow superior to her? Because she isn't a medical practitioner, but a writer? Doesn't her books about …?" He frowned, realizing he didn't know what Alyssa's books were about. He whipped out his cell, keyed in her name, then blinked back his shock. *Well I'll be damned.* "Never mind what they're about," he added, tucking his phone back in his pocket. "But is that what I'm hearing? From someone who is supposed to be a professional."

"Professional, not blind." Susan averted her gaze, and her alabaster skin flushed with a reddish color. "We have a business and an image to maintain. Why are you even entertaining having her around?"

"Because I can. And because Taj actually likes her, which is more than I can say for some people." Ahmad stole another glance at his son and Alyssa. "Not sure what level of professionalism you're embracing that would make you utter such low-minded things, but your statements say more about you than they ever will about her. Feel free to skip lunch."

Her lips twitched, and she glared openly at Alyssa. "No, I'll be there."

"See you then." He moved around a bench, aiming in the direction of his son.

Her hand snaked out, and she gripped his arm again, holding him in place. "I don't get a good feeling about this."

"You don't have to," he replied, extracting himself from her hold.

The moment Susan had been introduced to him at Durabia Medical Hospital, she had clung to him as though he was the last available man in a country where men outnumbered women two to one. He couldn't figure out what it was about him that made her so persistent that they move a business relationship in a direction that made absolutely no sense to him. But his investors, who were unsettled by the fact he was a single man, encouraged him to humor her. Her attachment was no laughing matter.

Alyssa looked up the moment he made it a few inches from where they were situated under a date palm tree.

"You need to get him the Sing, Spell, Read, and Write method," she suggested.

Taj swept past Ahmad to where his mother, Lauren, sat on a nearby wooden bench finding the whole exchange between Susan and Ahmad humorous. Taj leaned into her, showing her the page with his writing.

"You might have to find it on a resale site since they don't make it anymore," Alyssa said.

"And that will bring him up to speed with his studies?"

"He'll do well with this particular method." She gestured toward the tablet with the other work that Taj had done in the short time they'd been together. "My daughter certainly did."

"Your daughter?" He peered over her head, noticing that Susan lingered on the outskirts of the entrance pretending not to be watching the interaction, but her scowl gave it all away. "Did she come with you?"

"No, she wasn't able to. I ... I haven't seen or heard from her in years," she confessed, and there was a glint of sadness in her eyes. "Her father took her to Cuba and never returned."

"So sorry to hear that," he said, kicking himself for questioning something that would cause her pain. He wondered if she was aware that she wore her emotions like a garment. Maybe it was the reason she embraced writing in the first place.

"You are too kind." Her smile returned, and the sadness dissipated as fast as it appeared. "He wanted to punish me for leaving him. No greater way to do that than by taking the only person I ever loved."

Ahmad settled into the space beside her. "Have you ..."

She inhaled and let out her breath slowly. "Exhausted every dime I had back then on private investigators."

"Bounty hunters?"

"Did that too," she said, shifting to face him. "Even took a second mortgage on my home, which had been paid off. No one could find them. Either one of them. Especially given Cuba's contentious relationship with America."

His gaze landed on the tablet again. Her penmanship was beautiful and even in most places, but in other areas the ink had smeared, making the letters unrecognizable. "Thank you for accepting our offer for lunch. I appreciate what you've done with my son today. Of all the people I took him to for help, not one recognized that it's *how* he sees things that's the issue, and not that he can't read. They made him feel ... deficient, but today he feels excited and hopeful."

"My pleasure," she said, throwing a glance at Susan, whose eyes shot daggers in their direction. "Looks like someone has an issue with that lunch invite."

Ahmad followed her line of vision, realizing that Susan's quest for them to become something more than business partners ended the moment her true thoughts leaked from her mind and trickled past her lips.

The other partners were just going to have to be upset because he wasn't about to humor her any longer. "She'll get over it," he said.

"Famous last words," Alyssa whispered, causing unease to slither up his spine.

# Chapter 2

*They released Dippin' from prison today. He's coming for you.*

The early morning phone call from his brother passing along a message from someone in a place that Rahm had put in his rearview mirror, still disturbed him. Dippin' would be on probation and somewhere in downstate Illinois. He couldn't dwell on it now. So many other pressing matters demanded his attention. Like the fact that his main guest had been missing in action for a few hours.

"Auntie, how are you going to come all this way, then kick me to the curb to get some writing done?" He pressed the cell to his ear, grabbed his MacBook, and left the conference room on the way to his next meeting with the Kings of the Castle. "And now you're meeting up with some strangers for lunch. You don't know any folks here; you only touched down a few hours ago."

Alyssa chuckled, and Rahm, from the sound, knew he was in trouble. "Well, a certain nephew of mine left me to my own devices because he had an important meeting that came up with the … what did you call them?"

"Kings of the Castle." He laughed because he didn't know if she was deliberately forgetting or was still incensed that those powerful men were the reason he was leaving America behind. They also factored into his name change from Hiram to Rahm, a spiritual thing on his part. "You're never going to remember."

"Yes, *those* people," Alyssa said, and her tone was dry. "Don't trip. You know how I am when I'm in my writing cave. You missed your opportunity, my brother."

Rahm stood outside Sheikh Kamran and Sheikha Ellena's office building. The tallest building in the world, even though there was a "spire" dispute with the neighboring country of Dubai, that also tried to claim the title. He had a few minutes before his next meeting started, so he walked down the sidewalk and settled on a bench in the shade.

"And who are these people you're having lunch with?" Rahm opened the lid on his MacBook, ignoring the come hither glances from women who were close by. "I need to check them out."

"The father's name is Ahmad Maharaj," she said, adding a loud sigh. "His ex-wife, son, and business partner will be there, too. It should be safe enough."

"Give me a second, let me run a check on him." He keyed in the man's name. "I'm also going to send this to Kelly, my personal assistant, so she can do a more extensive probe on him."

"Personal assistant," she quipped. "Oh, so you have it like that?"

"Well, being connected to royalty has its privileges." Rahm let out an ear-splitting whistle. He'd found some good intel. "Oh, this dude is on fire. He's worth millions, and he's related to my boss. He might be all right."

"Yes, I was trying to tell you," she said.

"Still don't see why you have to ditch me for them," he mumbled, wishing he'd be there with her to feel out her lunch companions.

"And exactly how long is this meeting of yours supposed to last, nephew?"

He shifted past a group of businessmen as he stepped back inside the building. "Well, see, what had happened was—"

"Right. You don't know." Her laughter tinkled down the line, mingling with his. "Well, my empty stomach is not going to hang around for a maybe when there's a sure thing on the table."

"Oh, that's cold, Auntie," he said, glancing at the woman walking his way who looked a lot like the love of his life. "Take the dagger out of my heart."

"Well, make me a better offer for tomorrow."

"Why can't we catch up at dinner?" Rahm asked, setting the lock screen on his computer, then making his way to the food bar to find something for his own rumbling stomach. She may have already had her fill, but he still wanted to take her someplace nice.

"See, what had happened was ..." she hedged, using his earlier words.

"Aw man, you have a date for dinner, too?"

"Well, it's not exactly dinner, so ..."

"Dang, Auntie," he teased, grateful she couldn't see his scowl. "You sure do get around."

"Hey! You know what? You're not too old for me to put over my knee and spank that ass."

"Here we go with the threats," he said, laughing.

Rahm bypassed the meager offerings of the food bar and headed for the conference room, certain there would be a mouthwatering spread since Shaz would be at the meeting. That man's appetite was a legend unto itself.

"How about breakfast tomorrow?" she tossed out.

"Sounds like a plan. How do you like Durabia so far? You know, the parts of it you've seen while being a social butterfly and all that."

"Handle your business, nephew, and I'll meet up with you in the morning."

He placed his MacBook on the credenza, glad he followed his first mind because the buffet looked amazing. He snatched up a Samosa— a spicy potato-filled pastry that he was fast coming to love, since Shaz favored East Indian food for nearly every meeting. "Well, can I at least ask you who you're hanging out with tonight?"

"No, that's grown folks' business."

"Auntie, how can I keep you safe if you're all out here doing undercover stuff?" He stepped aside for two women who had tipped in and were loading up on the selections, knowing they weren't supposed to be in the room. "I'm not feeling this at all. Hey …" He put his focus on the brunette who had about a week's worth of food on two plates.

"Taking enough for the whole office?" he said, gesturing to her full hands.

"We won't tell if you won't," she teased.

"Difference is, I'm actually supposed to be in here," he told the woman, and the other one standing behind her grimaced and started sliding the one plate she held back onto the table. "Oh, don't put it back now. If you're busted, might as well make it worth it."

"I'll be fine, nephew," his aunt said, bringing him back to the current focus. "I know what I'm doing. It's a private event, and I've been to one in the States. It's safe. Trust me."

Trust her? He did. Everyone else—all these strangers she'd be with—were suspect. His Aunt was the only one, besides his mother, who believed he was innocent; the only one. His mother, though, hurt his heart when she refused to believe that Cain, her youngest son, had something to do with Rahm being framed for attempted murder. One admission of the truth and the case would have been settled in Rahm's favor.

"You took care of me all those years I was away." He piled on the rice dish, vegetables, and the sauce-covered entrée as the two women tipped out of the room with a conspirator's nod in his direction. "This is my turn to make sure you're straight."

"I appreciate it, my only nephew."

"Auntie, I'm not your only nephew."

"Well, you're the only one I claim," she shot back.

Yes, his Aunt was Team Rahm all the way and would never forgive Cain for what he had done. Neither would Rahm.

"And I'm beginning to think the main reason you want me over here is because of my peach cobbler," she teased, chuckling.

"Facts!" Rahm laughed as he disconnected the call, knowing she'd be all right, despite her "covert" activity. She could handle whatever came her way, but he still made a mental note to put a security tail on her at some point.

He turned his attention to a more pressing matter.

*They released Dippin' from prison today. He's coming for you.*

His brother, Cain, added another warning, "You need to come home and deal with this."

"Dippin'" was a cellmate when Rahm was serving time in Menard. The man had been given that name because he was always "dipping" into conversations that didn't concern him. He was already hated because he'd been sentenced for the types of crime even criminals hated. Prisoners didn't gel with creeps—those who were convicted of sexual crimes.

Creeps were those innocent-looking men—possibly six-foot-three, solid muscles, green or blue eyes, with shoulder-length or well-styled hair. The type who could get any woman they wanted. Those guys who weren't bad looking by reasonable standards. Yet, the games they played in hurting women were a mental thing. The idea of taking something that didn't belong to them appealed most.

Rahm was locked up with folks who were in for DUI's. The rest were sex cases and murders; snitches and such, and those who were in on child porn charges.

Dippin' had been arrested for an attack on his ex girlfriend. He had beaten her within an inch of her life, raped, and then strangled her with a shoestring. Dippin' said it was her ex who committed the crime. The jury didn't believe him. Neither did Rahm.

People serving time with him came from everywhere in the State of Illinois—Dekalb, Chicago, Peoria, Kankakee, and all over. Inmates gravitated to groups they were more familiar with, making prison life a territorial existence.

When someone like Dippin', who didn't come from Chicago, slid into a group of people with a conversation that started with, "Do you know what a Chicago high-five is?", he raised their hackles.

The first thought that came to mind was, *you're not from Chicago, so why do you have the Windy City all in your mouth?*

The next thing Dippin' said sealed his fate. "It's when two men rape a woman while giving each other a high-five."

Many levels exist to an ass whipping. The kind reserved for men in the family who got out of line. A decent ass whipping, where no one was trying to kill them. Maybe break a rib or two, but definitely not trying to kill anyone. And everyone lived to see another day.

When some of the Chicago inmates heard what Dippin' had put out there, they laid him on the bottom bunk, tied him up, and left the cell open for everyone to come in and put a hurting on his ass. When lights out came around, Rahm told him, "Now you know what your victim felt like."

Dippin' took weeks to recover and at no time did Rahm lift a finger to help, no matter how much he pleaded.

Evidently, Dippin' had taken that personally.

*They released Dippin' from prison today. He's coming for you.*

*Chapter 3*

Ahmad's home was immaculate. In fact, it deserved a spot on the cover of *Better Homes and Gardens* or some other high-end magazine that showcased the lives of the rich and famous. The perfectly manicured lawn accentuated the expansive house, with a gorgeous pool that spanned the house's entire length. His marble terrace and porch were seamlessly connected to the adjacent beach. So many windows graced the building, Alyssa wondered if he had a crew come out to clean them daily.

"Stay and enjoy the pool or the beach. Maybe you can get in some writing," Ahmad said, gesturing to the three cabanas that would provide shade from the heat of the Durabian sun.

"No, I can't stay any longer," Alyssa replied, after a meal of grilled salmon, asparagus, cucumber Caprese salad, and pistachio baklava. All under the observant eyes of Susan Abbott. Lauren, Ahmad's ex, seemed to enjoy the discomfort that Alyssa caused Susan. There had to be a story behind that. "I have to go back to my hotel and get ready for my event tonight."

"And what event is that?" Ahmad asked and narrowed his gaze on her to the point where she wondered if something in her voice had given away the specifics of the party.

"I'd rather not say."

Ahmad's eyebrow shot up. "There's not much going on in Durabia that we don't know about … unless it's not a public affair."

"I mean—never mind." Her gaze darted to every person sitting at the table as her leg bounced.

"No, tell me."

"It's a Bliss event." Her cheeks heated and she was sure they turned just the slightest shade of pink.

"What's that?"

"It's a …" She inhaled, glanced at Lauren and Susan, who waited for the answer. "It doesn't matter."

"I'll take you," Ahmad said, as if that sealed the matter.

"Wait, now you're providing personal escort services?" Susan interjected, her fork landing on the plate with a loud clatter.

Taj flinched at the sudden sound and shared a speaking glance with his mother, who exhaled her impatience.

"I'm going to need you to keep your nose out of my business and keep it squarely pointed on yours." Ahmad released his words in the direction of the woman who clearly needed to buy a clue or a vowel, whichever helped her get the message. "Alyssa, can you join me in my office for a few minutes?"

Alyssa stood and said, "Good night, Lauren and Taj. Oh …" she glanced at Susan. "Sorry, what was your name again?"

Susan's blue eyes narrowed to slits at the slight.

"Good night, Alyssa," Lauren said in a voice that was warm and sincere. "See you again soon."

"Soon?" Susan's head whipped toward Ahmad. "What's that supposed to mean?"

"Alyssa's agreed to work with Taj for the next ten days while he's here," Ahmad replied, taking the last sip of his spiced mojito.

"That's not possible," Susan shot back. "You're leaving in two days."

Lauren gave a half-smile and mischief twinkled in her green eyes. "Oh no, darling, we'll be here a little longer."

Susan's expression could only be summed up in one word—crestfallen.

Ahmad and Alyssa moved past the formal living area, the study, and down the spiral staircase into the lower level space where the décor screamed his style. He had stamped his personality onto the room in the cool sea colors and backdrop and the simple, but expensive furniture.

"I'm still interested in that event you're attending," he said, stopping just inside the door.

"Why is it your concern?" she shot back, tightening the hold on her purse strap. She took a step back, unnerved by the intensity in his eyes. Plus, his proximity made her nervous.

"I'm telling you that Durabia is not the type of place that has secrecy surrounding events. Unless it's *El Zalaam*, and that's not a place a woman would go into, unless she's working. And I don't think you do that kind of work." Ahmad held her gaze with a steady glare. "What is a Bliss event, Alyssa?"

She didn't answer, so he whipped out his cell and keyed in something. Alyssa averted her gaze, thinking he had a nerve to mention the place he had a moment ago. Even without him saying so, she knew it was a place of ill repute.

"I will accompany you to the event," Ahmad said after the silence had held court long enough.

"That's not necessary," Alyssa responded, wishing he'd get out of her business, the same way he wanted what's her face to stay out of his.

Her eyes darted toward the ceiling and the sound of heels clicking against the marble. Silence descended as the person made it to the staircase and paused.

"It is not a request," Ahmad countered. "You are going into a place with a strange group of people for some clandestine activity that you can't share. I'm almost certain your beloved nephew you spoke of during dinner doesn't know about it either. In the Middle East, women go missing just as easily as they do in America. I simply want to ensure your safety. That is all."

Alyssa mulled that over. He did have a point. Rahm wasn't aware of the details of this excursion, and he didn't need to be. He had given her an all-expense paid vacation for her to see what Durabia had to offer before she decided to relocate permanently. Since he'd been promoted to a Knight of the Castle and these new opportunities opened up, she had taken him up on the offer. She loved everything that she'd seen so far. "You'll escort me to the house and leave, right?" she asked.

"That is the plan," Ahmad responded.

Something about his tone and the immediacy of the answer did not ring true. She stared into his eyes trying to figure out his possible motive. She still didn't understand why he seemed so concerned about her plans. From what Rahm had told her, Durabia was one of the safest countries in the world.

"They're strangers?" he asked. "All of these people?"

Ahmad frowned and tipped his head to one side. Then he pointed up, letting her know someone was eavesdropping.

"Except one. The host. Everyone else is from different places across the world."

Ahmad pondered that for several moments. "You're a beautiful, passionate, amazing woman."

His comment took her aback. "What do you know about my passion?"

"It's in your writing," he replied. "Any woman who can zone out in the middle of a busy park and be so focused on something that brings up such strong emotions is passionate. It doesn't take much to figure that out." He motioned for her to move farther into the office and closed the door. "These are people you don't know, but you're about to share an important part of your life with them. I just want to know … why this? Why not find someone you care about and have this kind of experience?"

She wondered what kind of answer would suffice. Only the truth. His genuine concern warranted that. Ahmad gestured for them to take a seat at the round conference table in the center of the office.

Portraits of Taj and Lauren hung on the walls. She realized then that Taj had his thick, silky hair, olive skin, and soulful eyes. He'd grow to be tall and handsome like his father.

"Tony was the last man I was with, and I miss him so much it hurts.

We hadn't made it to the good wood yet," she said, her voice filled with raw emotion, and eyes glazed over with tears.

His perplexed expression forced her to continue, "Oh, no, I don't mean making love. I mean the best part of the relationship." She sighed, and there was a world of pain in the sound. "I didn't have to pretend with him. Wig or weave. Natural, straight hair, or whatever. He loved me for me. Rolls, cellulite, breasts not quite where they used to be. Love handles being more like bridges. None of that mattered to him. It mattered to me."

"Papa?" Taj's voice penetrated the office, interrupting their conversation. He cracked open the door and peered in before running straight into Alyssa's arms. Ahmad let him have a few moments, then said, "Please return to your mother. I will come up shortly to tuck you in."

"Yes, Papa," Taj said with a sour face as he pointed upward, signaling that he also knew that Susan was not supposed to be creeping nearby. He moved toward the door, then came back for one final hug from Alyssa before closing the door behind him.

Ahmad gestured for her to go on.

"Unconditional love," she said once they were alone again. "Never had that before. I kept attracting men who affirmed what I felt about myself. I didn't even have a floor-length mirror in my house. Tony bought me one. I still have it. Every day, I stand before it and try to tell myself that I am beautiful. Even today, it's still a struggle." Her voice broke, and she found a pointed interest in the wrought iron airplane wing desk across the room, wanting to avoid seeing the pity in his eyes. She chuckled a little, but there was no happiness in the sound. "One would think at my age that wouldn't be the case. It took me two years of speaking intentions every day, claiming what I wanted to experience in an intimate relationship, to bring Tony into my life."

Ahmad handed her a tissue for the single tear that fell from her eye.

"He never let me see myself any way but beautiful."

He touched her elbow, and when she didn't flinch, he wrapped her in his arms, as if trying to ease her pain.

Alyssa stayed there a few moments and then sat back. She took a few moments then picked up where she left off. "After he was killed, I didn't even tune my lips up to ask God to send me another man. I didn't write any more intentions. The lesson I learned is one that will be with me for the rest of my life." She placed her hand over her heart, as though it could slow the rapid beats. "God sent me someone who would love me for me. The problem is that even now, I don't love me for me.

"I've taken all these years to have a love affair with myself. Now, I'm ready to try—put my toe in the water. Maybe welcome someone else's touch, possibly be intimate again. This,"—she pointed to his cell and the search he'd executed,—"is the best way. A Bliss Event is a safe place, with people who are playing by the same set of rules. But it's not something that everyone understands." She crossed one leg over the other. "I like that idea. Like I said, everyone is playing by the same set of rules."

"Makes sense," Ahmad responded, sliding his thumb across the screen to lock his phone. "Half of the world's problems arise because everyone's not on the same page. Raised different, not always taught to respect other cultures, then turned loose on the world with no concept of what other people require and no empathy or understanding as a frame of reference." He leaned forward, close enough for her to feel his concern. "And you said these are not people you met in the States?"

"No, only the host, Charli," she admitted. "I met a man there who caught my interest, but he only had eyes for two other women."

"At the same time?" His eyes widened to the size of saucers.

"No," she replied, laughing. "The first one married a Bollywood superstar who became a popular singer."

"Devesh Maharaj?" His response came in seconds.

"Yes, him." Alyssa smiled, wondering how he could know. "The other woman paired up with a wealthy East Indian businessman."

His brow lifted as though finding that especially interesting. "And they were Black women?"

"Yes."

"Is that a going thing now?" He studied her, wearing a neutral expression. "Black women with Indian men?"

She placed a dramatic hand just above her breasts. "Well, there's always been a saying that Black folks have Indian blood in their family."

"They don't mean my kind of Indian when they say that." Ahmad chuckled, and she joined him.

"I'm just stating the facts," she said with a shrug.

He brought his laughter under control. "I would like to go inside and check everything out."

"You can't," she said. "You have to be registered and vetted by the host."

"We'll see." He picked up his phone and punched some digits before laying it down again.

She peered at him, "Why are you so curious? I'm not inviting you."

"I'm intrigued by the concept of an event that's putting people in touch with their needs, and things in perspective. Tomorrow, are you still able to spend a little time here with Taj?"

"I'll see what I can do," she said, avoiding his intense gaze. "I was hoping to get a few chapters in."

"You can write here while you're with him. I'll let you use my office."

She adjusted the purse strap over her shoulder. "Because he's so excited right now, your son requires my undivided attention. I can't do any writing then."

"Yes, he's fascinated with you," Ahmad said.

When a micro-frown crossed her face, he winked. "Well, how else would you describe it?"

"I'd say he's more enthusiastic about learning because it's not so much of an uphill battle. I'm happy to help him progress."

"Does that mean you'll come?" Ahmad asked, wearing a smile she found all too attractive.

She got to her feet, willing herself not to be distracted by his expectant gaze and the glossy goatee she badly wanted to touch. "I'll try to make that happen."

# Chapter 4

Susan studied herself in the floor-length mirror in the bedroom she had in the upper level of Ahmad's home. She plucked at the creases in her pants, then turned to admire her small waist and tight bottom. Surely any man would fall on his knees to have her. She fluffed the rich blond curls and narrowed her crystal-blue eyes to slits as she ran a finger over the beginnings of a faint laugh line and frowned.

*One Botox trip to Dani in Beverly Hills can take care of that.*

Then she remembered that leaving the States under the cover of darkness was her only choice. Her daddy could only fix so much, and thanks to the woman she hated more than anyone else in the world, he no longer held the same power and connections. Yes, she had made a few bad investments, judgment calls, and took the wrong people at their word. So what, she'd made a few bad calls during medical procedures and had been found criminally negligent of one and was indicted for several others. Sometimes giving favors to her father's friends had its advantages.

Now she was on the other side of the world trying to fit in with a bunch of sand dwellers. The trip meant a chance to regroup and think up a strategy that didn't involve her wallowing in prison wearing stripes or eating her meals from a metal tray.

The thought of being cooped up in a cell with some sloppy woman who smelled like piss or rancid cooking oil, made her stomach lurch. It never ceased to amaze her how many women let themselves go, when all they had to do was push back from the table and walk around the block. More than once, she had to excuse herself from the examination room because the patient came in with her hair teased into oblivion or dyed dollar bill green or purple. The ones who bleached the ends of their hair made her laugh the most. To her, they looked like the two-tone batteries sealed in hard plastic that required a chainsaw to cut through. No class. Like that Alyssa person who reminded Susan a great deal of the woman who had stolen her ex-husband. She never saw that woman coming. She did see this one, though. And Ahmad was ripe for the plucking. Lauren, his ex, that seemed to have an emotional tie to him was nearly out of the picture; if she'd just die already.

Susan unbuttoned her lavender linen suit jacket and cupped her left breast. She was still firm in all the right places, with no stretch marks or tell-tale signs of a pregnancy that would not only ruin her figure but also tie her to a screaming, sniveling creature that could drain her finances and dog her steps until the day she died.

Alyssa crossed her mind once more, and she frowned. The wench had bested her by getting to Ahmad through his son. He hated having this particular fight again. Obviously, she was looking for a free ride, and he took the bait faster than a catfish went after squid. She wasn't even pretty. And—

The phone rang, interrupting her mini tirade. Susan straightened her jacket, then breezed over to the bed to extract the cell from her purse.

"This is Susan."

"Tell me more about this expatriate that is sniffing around my brother."

Susan grinned as Ahmad's brother's thick accented voice filled her ear. If Jameel Maharaj wasn't already taken, Susan would've tried her luck with him. He was as attractive as any of the Maharaj men. She perched on the ottoman, ready to spill the little dirt she knew.

"Well, it's like I said, she was all over him making a fool of herself. She had the audacity to turn on the tears at one point, and your brother bit into that like a kid snacking on a candy bar." She couldn't help snarling, "Your nephew seemed to like her well enough. Maybe entirely too much. All I'm saying is that Taj is impressionable, and she is a stranger, low class and ex—"

Susan heard other voices in the background before he replied, "I understand the situation. Their being here has caused us enough trouble," Jameel growled. "All it took was one royal to buck tradition, and everyone else is following suit. Honor is not a thing to be trifled with. Just look at the news in America. Crime is horrendous. What if they bring that foolishness here?"

Susan went back to the mirror, grinned at her reflection, and twirled her curls, loving the stark transformation from brunette to blonde, an effort to change her appearance. The moment she had Ahmad in line and down the aisle, she would have no worries about her status back in America. That indictment would go away, and she'd be securely under his protection. Unfortunately, he came with a lot more strings attached— an ex-wife who was on her way out permanently, a precocious little boy that she'd send packing off to boarding school the minute the ink was dry on the marriage certificate. Not to mention Ahmad's love for this god-forsaken hell of glorified sand dwellers. He didn't realize it, but he was going to be transplanted back to the civilized world—the American heartland—in no time flat.

"What does this woman do for a living? Is she a learned woman such as yourself?"

The woman's voice behind Jameel grew louder, and a man also joined the conversation. "Hardly, I'm a Doctor of Medicine. She scribbles on a sheet of paper, and your brother fell all over himself. I doubt if she even has a degree. She couldn't possibly be on the same level as us. Very few of them are, you know."

Jameel shouted something in his native tongue before he returned to the call. "Did my brother say where he was going with the woman this evening?"

Susan's smile faded a little as she remembered how he left her at the table with his ex-wife and son. Both of them stared at her as if she was the interloper.

"Something about a Bliss Party. I hear those things are pretty risqué on a good day." Susan opened the mini-fridge and poured herself a glass of Pinot Grigio.

"The idea that she could be exposing him to dishonor is of some concern."

"Well, I figured you might want to know."

She moved the phone from her mouth and took a few sips of the refreshing white wine. Moving the phone back, she continued, "I mean, after all, he is a man of prominence. The last thing he needs is the appearance of impropriety. Hasn't your family suffered enough from those two scandals?"

Susan bit down on her bottom lip and waited for his response. In truth, she didn't know anything about the Bliss Parties, but if they were anything like the Lock and Key events she attended back in the day, then there was bound to be someone on all fours in one of the rooms.

She refilled her glass with the last of the wine and perched on the ottoman.

"Well, I will have a talk with my brother, and I will send you someone to help with your little problem," Jameel conceded. "You have been a friend to this family, and we remember our friends."

Susan could barely suppress the giggle of glee rising in her chest. *Alyssa, your days are numbered, sweetheart. Step aside and let a real woman get to work. You can be my maid if you want. Maybe you can keep house, clean my shoes, and take care of that bothersome child of his. Yes, that will work. You can live out the rest of your days here with my stiletto heel on your neck. Right where your kind belongs, under my foot.*

She waited for the line to go dead before she preened in her mirror once more.

*Game. Set. Match, to the beautiful blonde in the mirror.*

# Chapter 5

Fresh off his disappointment at not being able to personally welcome his aunt to Durabia, Rahm struggled to absorb another blow.

"I'm not moving to the middle east."

Rahm sprawled on the king-sized bed in his tri-level home on Durabia's riverside with an amazing view of the towering skyscrapers that made up the city's skyline. The seven-bedroom luxury home he requested was still under construction because it was being redesigned. Everyone important to him would live comfortably in separate suites. He thought it would be finished in time for his aunt's visit, but they ran into a few glitches, and he had to put her up in a hotel.

"Marilyn, how can you lay this on me right now?" Rahm asked, filtering through every scenario that he might have missed seeing this coming. "We've already discussed this, and you know the game plan. I have several businesses starting here. There's too much going on in America right now, and the Castle's interests are now split between both countries."

"I thought I could do it, Rahm," she said in a defeated tone. "I really did. But my family is here."

"They're only a plane ride away." He sat up and slid to the edge of the bed, trying not to let frustration have a front seat in his emotional wheelhouse.

"And I'm not too keen on being taken care of by a man," she admitted. "I've been on my own since I was fourteen." Fourteen, because her stepfather believed that where her mother's bedroom duties ended, her daughter should pick up the slack.

"I'm aware of that, babe." He heard the rustling of papers on her end as he stared at his feet. "You already have a position waiting for you in one of Sheikha Ellena's companies. That will be your money. And there is no way I'm letting you pay any bills in our home. That's what a grown-ass man is supposed to do. Provide. Your money is for you to do whatever you want."

"You want children," she countered, obviously not absorbing the words he just spoke because they didn't fit her new narrative. "I'm way past time for that. I have two grown daughters. I am not rewinding the parent clock to zero."

Rahm thought the children part of their argument was the least of the issue. With Dippin' gunning for him, every woman close to him was in danger. "Now, I'll have to come back to the States next week to bring my mother. She was supposed to come with you because I wanted all of the people I love in a place where I could keep them safe, and we'd build a new life."

"I'm sorry, Rahm," she whispered after several moments of silence. "I truly am. You're bringing your family with us, but mine are here. One of my daughters is getting married, and then I'll have grandchildren and all of that. I don't want to miss out on those aspects of my life. You're just starting yours and mine is at a different stage."

Rahm rubbed his temples. That same old argument again. The difference in their ages and her perceived thoughts of what he wanted, instead of what he actually said. "I offered to bring your daughters too. I know what it means to have family close. You are my family. The Kings, Knights, and the Queens are my family now. My mother sacrificed a lot for me during those years I was incarcerated. My aunt, who is here checking things out, is also someone I wanted here with me. A fresh start for everyone."

"My daughters do not wish to move to the Middle East," she shot back. "And they've made me understand how difficult it is for women there."

"The Kings, Khalil, and Sheikh Kamran are doing their level best to change how Durabia treats women and people of color." He walked to the mini bar and pulled out a water bottle, downing the contents in two gulps.

"The Sheikh is changing things here to make this a better place for all people—ours included. The kind of place America should be but is too caught up in discrimination, segregation, bias against women, and elitism to accomplish. He's trying to make beautiful things happen here. And I want all of us to be a part of that."

"Rahm, I understand," she countered. "But our relationship was a fantasy to begin with. I'm nearly fifteen years older than you are. I'm on the 'almost down for the count' part of my life. You're on the 'let's get ready to rumble' part of yours."

Always speaking as if she had one foot in the grave and the other kicking down death's door. Good Lord!

"Age wasn't a problem when I was between your thighs bringing you to not only your first set of multiple orgasms, but your best," he shot back, ignoring her shocked gasp. "Age wasn't a problem when I perceived that something wasn't quite right with your youngest daughter's relationship with her father. Age wasn't a problem when we figured out a plan to save Jaidev when the place you worked for was trying to shut him down. Marilyn, age wasn't a problem when you told me you loved me." He tossed the bottle in the trash, wishing he could find something to throw against the wall instead. "I'm not too young to experience the life we could have. I'm not ready for us to end before we begin."

She was silent so long, he wasn't sure if she was hurt or angry. Then, she simply said, "I'm not moving to Durabia."

This was the worst news possible. His best relationship ever was imploding because of things beyond his control. The second such issue that happened since he walked out of Menard. Brittany, his ex, who had "held it down for him" while he was away, had changed drastically when he came home. She had a checklist. Married. White picket fence. Two-point-five children. Rahm surmised that she was only trying to help him simply so he could help her.

Six months after release, they were in two different places fundamentally. She was anal, close-minded, and could be quite cold. His character was free-spirited, happy to have endless opportunities before him, and empathetic to a point. He enjoyed being around people—especially friends and family. She was more like "fuck everybody. Well, except you. I kinda like you." If a situation didn't benefit her, she wanted no part of it.

When Rahm walked into a room, he spoke to everyone. She walked in, and her face was already set to "mean mug." Problems that should've been resolvable were so bad, he moved out twice then returned to apologize. He stayed because of an obligation that he probably shouldn't have felt. Especially given the fact that rumors had swirled that Brittany had slid into Cain's bed when Rahm had only been in that prison van for one hour. Even when he was inside, she didn't call consistently, which he couldn't understand. How hard could it be to hold a conversation with someone for thirty minutes, once every few days?

Loyalty dictated that he tough the relationship out as long as he could. And he did. When he landed the position at Chetan Rehabilitation and Restorative Care, things between them went so far south, any feelings he had were still somewhere near the equator. Then Marilyn Spears came into his life. Totally by accident. She worked for the bureau gunning to shut down Jaidev Maharaj's medical center, after the place came under fire. A coma patient wound up pregnant after being in the facility for twelve months. The story developed quickly because the media became involved and discovered that the male employees were all ex-felons. Jaidev, a member of the Kings of the Castle, believed in giving second chances. Rahm, and his fellow co-workers, certainly appreciated the confidence.

The outcome brought several powerful things—Marilyn into his life, his record expunged, and a coveted position as a Knight of the Castle, which eventually led to a wonderful series of opportunities in Durabia.

Marilyn, a woman fifteen years older, was perfect because she was established, seasoned, and didn't play the games played by some of the other women he'd come across. Women with that entitled, or "you owe me" persona. Meaning they wanted Rahm to make up for things that happened to them in their past. They brought all of the past and those demands to the table when Rahm had just arrived and didn't even know what was being served.

That's why some older men were pulling for young girls with no life experience because they would get all of the benefits, but none of the "chip" on the shoulder.

Once, in the heat of an argument, Rahm had to tell his mate, "Don't come down on someone who hasn't done anything to you. I can't shoulder the cross for the sins of the men before me."

Rahm hadn't realized he said that part aloud until Marilyn spoke.

"I never asked you to shoulder anything that happened to me before you came on the scene," she snapped. "I was doing just fine."

Mad at himself for thinking out loud and for her non-progressive attitude, he punched the air. "If by fine, you mean working a nine to five," Rahm said, "saving for retirement, being at your family's beck and call, and barely existing, call me when you want something more for yourself."

# Chapter 6

"Oh, my word, is that …" Charli's bright blue eyes opened wide with wonder. The Bliss event's host was a level-headed, but free-spirited woman—sexy and sultry, and the type of red-head that made men lose their natural minds.

"It is," Sherry, a leggy brunette drawled, sauntering up next to Charli, her intense gaze locked on Ahmad who was headed in their direction. "Did you come to join us?"

"No, I simply wanted to make sure my guest was safe."

Charli gave him a lengthy once-over. "Well, come on in," she purred. "See for yourself."

Alyssa gave him a warning look that made him smile as he ignored its meaning and said, "Don't mind if I do."

"That's not how you said this works," a tall blonde admonished, amidst a flurry of activity and thrum of conversation that escalated the moment people laid eyes on Ahmad. "Everyone is supposed to preregister. You vet all of the guests before they arrive."

"Everyone knows who Ahmad Maharaj is," Charli said, placing her hand on his sculpted chest. His face had been on billboards and commercials due to being the face of the Durabia Medical Symposium that brought in top doctors from all over the world.

"He needs to pay the required fee, of course. But he is welcome to stay …" She shifted her gaze to Alyssa. "This way he'll know you're all right, since he seems *sooooo* concerned."

The fact that Alyssa didn't want him there was a challenge unto itself, but he should also be aware that he shouldn't want to piss her off to the point that she wouldn't join him in the morning. Taj required her more than Ahmad needed to satisfy his curiosity. "I will only stay for a short while, if you'll agree to come to breakfast."

"Breakfast?" Alyssa chirped.

Charli perked up and her brows danced. "See? She'll be home before midnight. Just like a modern-day Cinderella. Problem solved."

"You said this is a safe space," Alyssa tossed to Charli, feeling as if she wanted to back out of the evening's activities. "How can it be safe if you're letting random plus ones in?"

"Not so random if he came with you," she shot back with a saucy little wink. "We'll put it to a vote." Charli's voice carried across several connecting rooms, causing others to emerge from places where they were stationed to witness the new developments. "Everyone, we have someone who'd like to remain with us for only a *short* while. Permission to stay?"

She raised her hand, and every one of the women's hands went up—immediately. Every single one. The men shared a collective groan, then slowly, all but five gave their consent.

"See? Majority rules," Charli piped in with a flourish of her graceful hand. "Problem solved."

"Your favorite words," Alyssa mumbled.

Ahmad brushed past her and claimed an open seat on an ivory sofa. The only other vacant space in the place was next to him. The mellow R&B music playing in the background soothed Alyssa's nerves. She glanced out of the window at the night sky, then to the exquisite flooring while pondering her options.

She remained near the door, determined not to be in close proximity to a man who oozed sex appeal and caused her such angst. Not since

Tony had been in her life, had she felt anything for a man. Why him? And why now? She hadn't asked God to send her a man since perfection came in that six-foot-three, milk chocolate, chiseled man who loved her like no other. He set the bar so high that she was still high off the memories alone. But Ahmad … something about him put her panties and everything else in an uproar. Memories of love were nice, but they didn't warm her bed the way Tony had.

Ahmad waited several moments before patting the empty space and said, "I don't bite. Unless you're into that sort of thing."

She gave him the evil eye, then crossed the distance between them, sliding into the seat but making sure a few inches separated them. Even with the chatter and clinking glasses, she didn't miss his low throaty chuckle because it rankled her nerves.

The Opening Circle, where all the rules were laid out for strangers embarking on an unforgettable journey, began.

They remained on a sofa for a while, in a room filled with people who had come for one purpose—a Bliss Event, an extension of the Big Spoon-Little Spoon Party, the new wave of safe adult interaction. Everyone learned and played by identical rules during the four-hour time period. The word "no" was met with a comforting phrase, "Thank you for taking care of yourself."

"Rule one … garments stay on the whole time," their fiery-haired host explained.

"Rule two," Charli continued. "You don't have to physically connect with anyone at a Bliss Event. Ever."

One of the rules drifted into the forefront of Alyssa's mind because it was the most comforting of all. *If you agree to a request, say "Yes." If you are not willing to entertain a request, say "No." If you are on the fence, say "no". You always have the right to change your mind and are encouraged to do so.*

Alyssa welcomed the idea that the rules left no room for doubt. "Maybe" would be voiced as a "No." No quipping, no explanations, arguments, or persuasion—a simple "No," and the participant moved on with that confirming statement. True power lay in the person who respected the other's boundaries.

*Another rule ... you must ask permission and receive a verbal confirmation before putting your hands on anyone.*

Their first night of the Bliss Event was spent watching, instead of participating. Whether from the sofa, the balcony, or the kitchen, watching *is* participating according to their terms.

"In the States, what brought you to a place like this?" he asked after they returned to the living room where another couple was cuddled up on the sofa.

"I was having an affair."

"Excuse me?" Ahmad inched closer because the music was louder than when the event first started.

"I'm still having a love affair with myself. Trying new things, exploring ..." she explained while watching Charli sashay around the room making sure the guests were comfortable. She continued, avoiding his eyes. "I do things now that I'm close to pushing into my new age bracket that I wouldn't have done twenty years ago."

"Are men kind of intimidated by you, the books you write, the way you speak, and that you own your sexuality?" Ahmad asked.

"Boys yes, real men no," Alyssa replied. "Of course, I own my sexuality. No one else is renting it out right about now." Her gaze zoned in on two women conversing, their eyes were "speaking" love.

"Normally, women at this time of life are pushing to get married."

"No, I'm team fornication all the way," she confessed. "But I'm open to trying things that I wasn't before."

"What brought that on?" Ahmad asked, keeping his focus squarely on her no matter how many women tried to get his attention.

"My housekeeper. She had the keys to my place. One day she came early."

"Okay, I don't see a problem yet."

Alyssa turned her face toward his. "She came before I put the toys away."

Ahmad's eyes widened with shock and his lips turned up at the corners. "Okay, then *that's* a problem."

The sound of a woman's playful yelp caught her attention. "When I came home, and she stepped out of the elevator into the lobby and saw me," she said in that heavy accent, 'Miss Aleeeessa, I know why you no have boyfreeeend'." Alyssa couldn't help the laughter that spilled over.

"That's not funny," Ahmad said, wearing a slight smile.

"You have to admit, that was kind of funny," she replied, still laughing but also noticing the stares from some of the men in the room.

"Okay, maybe a little."

The men seemed almost hungry, and she didn't understand why, when there were so many gorgeous women to choose from.

"Back home, there's this newspaper called the Redeye, and they advertised Big Spoon-Little Spoon Parties. I thought, how desperate does a woman have to be to attend a party just to get her cuddle on? I've been celibate for six years now, after I lost the love of my life. And let me tell you, on a scale from one to ten, that brother was a good god-damn."

Ahmad held up six fingers, while simultaneously mouthing the words, "*Six.*"

She nodded. "Anyway, I went to this Big Spoon-Little Spoon Party, and I'm expecting it to be like the picture where everyone is all spooned up in a puppy pile and get to sleep peacefully with a few others. But it was a totally different experience."

More couples, some tourists, and other nationals continued to flow through the different rooms of the property. This was, by far, the largest event she had attended of this kind.

"My first Big Spoon-Little Spoon Party was the most intensely beautiful experience of my life. They told us the rules, we learned that no means no, and then let us out to play. People were on the mattress, on the couch, eating at the kitchen island. It's like a real party, and everyone kept their clothes on. At the first level, not everyone came for a hookup;

sometimes, it's all about healing," she explained.

"Yes, and for some it's all about the score," he said, looking over her shoulder.

Alyssa turned to find a group of men wearing designer pajamas, who had that polished look of the wealthy. They were talking amongst themselves but had trouble written all over them.

She turned assessing eyes on Ahmad as he drew her closer to his side.

*Chapter 7*

The breathtaking view of the palace never got old. The warmth and opulence of the gold and red hues accented everything and seemingly welcomed one home. The massive walls made Rahm feel like Jack in the giant's house. As soon as he entered the building, a staff member escorted him to Sheikh Kamran's office. The décor resembled the rest of the palace—everything extravagant and elegant. Unfortunately, this was also where he was presented with even more bad news.

"Why are they just telling me now," Rahm roared, unable to fathom something like this. "They waited until I made it all the way here. The shop is about to open, employees are all set to roll, and *now* they're saying the kind of business I want to open is against the law."

Sheikh Kamran Ali Khan, the ruler of Durabia, glanced at Jaidev Maharaj, Rahm's former boss. Both of them were tall with olive skin and dark hair; one was outfitted in a black designer suit and the other in a white dishdasha. Sheikh Kamran gazed at Rahm as he said, "It has always been against Muslim laws."

"But my shop will be in the Free Zone, and the laws are less strict."

"Yes, but this is something different," Sheikh Kamran countered.

Rahm squared his shoulders. "People let all of those other things fly, but they draw the line at tattoos. Is that what you're telling me?" He didn't care that the silence around them hinted that the staff outside had paused from their tasks at his tone, which might be seen as disrespectful in their eyes, but was strictly intended to make his point. The team of workers arranging food at the sideboard went still.

"There are so many changes happening in Durabia since Sheikh Kamran married Sheikha Ellena," Jai explained. "The Tribunal revisited some old customs, and we're dealing with the effects that so many interracial marriages are creating. Old fears are resurfacing, and right now this venue is being seen as one more thing against tradition. It's not a good time for you to open the shop. Please forgive the inconvenience."

"This is way more than simple inconvenience. Jai, I need you to go to bat for me the same way I did for you," Rahm said with a pointed look at his mentor. "The way we did when the State and media came all up in your grill about Temple winding up pregnant. You believed in us enough to hire us, even with the felonies on our records."

"Certain felonies," Jai clarified for Sheikh Kamran, who frowned upon hearing those words.

"Right, the *acceptable* ones," Rahm supplied, in a skeptical tone.

"We are not saying you cannot open at all," Sheikh Kamran explained in his lightly accented English. "We are just saying give it a little time and allow the nationals to become accustomed to the new norms. The Durabia Tribunal are setting some boundaries and standards now. Especially with the influx of international guests. We can revisit the tattoo shop." He motioned for his staff to leave the room after all the refreshments had been laid out.

"Some of my other businesses were going to be funded by profits from the shop."

"I will reimburse you for any inconvenience," Sheikh Kamran replied.

They waited until the last servant left the room before he continued the conversation. "I don't want your money," Rahm said. "I don't need a handout. This place, giving me opportunities, was supposed to be a hand up."

"Your position at Chetan is still available until this is all sorted out," Jai offered, trying to deescalate the situation.

"Is that what this is really about?" Rahm tugged at the crown crest cuff links he'd been given as a member of The Castle. He had taken to wearing suits like the other members, therefore the reason he had on one similar to Jai's.

"Watch it, Rahm, you're treading very close to disrespect," Jai snapped. "You know I supported your leaving."

His anger was evident as he paced in front of the Durabian flag situated in the corner of the office. "But you weren't all that happy about it, either."

"True, but I would never sabotage your efforts," he said, and his dark brown gaze narrowed on Rahm. "And I resent you insinuating such a thing."

Rahm took a breath and released it slowly. "You're right. My apologies, Jai."

Sheikh Kamran settled on the edge of the mahogany desk, his gaze on Jai. "You mentioned something that I am now understanding. You hired *prisoners* to work at your medical center?"

"Ex-felons," Jai said, taking the seat in front of the desk. "Men who had paid their debt to society."

"How did they end up being Knights?" he queried, his eyebrows drawing in with a quick flicker at Rahm. "I thought they were businessmen like you and the others."

Jai adjusted his seat, crossed his legs, and got comfortable. "They became Knights because they provide exemplary service to The Castle. Remember, they were the ones who covered your ass right here in Durabia when your family lost their minds."

"Truth," he said, but still seemed unsettled.

"So now you pick this time to be bothered by that." Rahm shook his head. "That's rich."

"No, simply, it is that others will see things a little differently. Especially the Tribunal—they do not know your history, Jai does," Sheikh Kamran replied. "And I know he is family and all, but I am the one who is catching flack for this influx of Americans who have become instant royalty.

A staff member entered, bringing water for Sheikh Kamran, Jai, and

Rahm. Once he completed his tasks, the Sheikh thanked and dismissed him.

Rahm weighed all sides, realizing this current action was not an act of inequity, nor was it rooted in malice. "What can I do to ease your mind?"

"You do not have to do anything. Jai says that you all are solid; I trust him, and I believe in what you have done for the kingdom."

"What can I do to put your mind at ease? Yours," Rahm repeated. "Not secondhand. Not 'I hope Jai's right.' Yours. Ask the question that will at least give you peace."

Sheikh Kamran turned his gaze on Jai, who nodded, before he put his focus back on Rahm. "All right, I would not have asked otherwise, but how did you end up in such a place?"

Rahm planted himself on the leather executive chair and waited for Jai to adjust so he was able to face both of them. "It was my friend's birthday," he said. "And we were hanging at a spot near North Avenue in Chicago. My brother, Cain, his girlfriend, Tammy, my homegirls, and ex-girlfriend were there." He shifted his gaze to Jai who nodded for him to continue. "One of the women who was with us double-parked in front of this dude's car, and he came out snapping. Tammy was holding a conversation with someone else when we heard the guy going off. My brother slid between them, and I said ... 'Who the hell are you talking to? You don't want that smoke'."

"Smoke?" Sheikh Kamran asked, looking to Jai for an explanation.

"Smoke," Jai said with a grin. "Physical heat on that ass."

"Right," Rahm said. "Then this guy came out of the club with his shirt off, kind of lit on something he'd taken."

"Lit?"

Jai lowered his head and chuckled as he explained, "Lit means high."

"Is there a thesaurus or something so I can learn to translate these things on my own?" Sheikh Kamran asked, his face a mask of concern.

"That's what you have me for, cousin," Jai quipped, laughing while Rahm shook his head.

"Right. Carry on," Sheikh Kamran said in a gesture that meant for Rahm to finish.

"And he sees us getting into it with his friend. From there it escalated all the way to him yelling, cursing, and calling us everything but a child of God. One of his friends came running up behind him and said, 'Dude, you can't mess with them. They're bigger than you. Unless you're ready to meet your maker, walk away'." Rahm paused in the middle of the story to gauge Sheikh Kamran's response. His facial reaction remained neutral, but at least he was following along. Jai had already heard the story when Rahm first came in for the interview to work at Chetan.

"That made the dude even angrier. Now none of that set me off, but I do remember that the moment he went in on Tammy, nearly put his hands on her. I wasn't going to let that ride. Especially since the dude had a weapon and was aiming to do something with it. The women with us were directly in his line of fire. So when he reached out to lay hands on Brittany and Tammy, we put in a little bit of work."

"Work?" Sheikh Kamran said, sighing before he glanced at Jai, who said, "Classic term for an ass whipping."

Rahm lowered his head and chuckled. "Yeah, that's one way of putting it. But like I said, we *put in that work*. And it would have stayed only *that work*. Except the party's promoter saw his friend had met with the ground and was kissing it like a long-lost lover. No one had called the police, everything happened so fast that no one had time.

"But this promoter flagged down the police who were cruising by. He didn't tell him the whole story. He pointed me out, and that's when the real fun began. His friend who started the whole thing should've been pulled in on charges, but unfortunately, that didn't happen. All the heat fell on me."

"That was truly unfortunate, and I regret that you lost so many years of your life for protecting the women who were in trouble," Sheikh Kamran said. He took a sip of water, and his gaze swept across Rahm as though studying him for the first time.

"Six years. They went harder on me because of my martial arts background."

"And no one found out about the weapon?" Sheikh Kamran asked, and Rahm loved the fact that the Sheikh had picked up on the major issue that the police didn't.

"That, and my brother were the two things that stood between me and freedom."

Jai and Sheikh Kamran passed a glance between them, one that Rahm didn't miss.

"Dude handed his weapon to someone who took it off the premises before I told the police that there was a gun in play they should be looking for. No one, not even my brother, fessed up to say they saw it."

"Your own brother?" Sheikh Kamran asked.

"Long story, not even worth sharing." Rahm took a long swallow of his water, but realized Sheikh Kamran might understand that level of ugliness. His brothers were next level of cutthroat. "But when he lied on the witness stand, that is what tipped the case away from me. Receiving a much lighter sentence and possibly no jail time at all depended on him." Rahm sat his bottle down, trying not to let any of the anger still burning inside him enter his voice. "So unfair when you know that you didn't begin the fight and some promoter dude pulled law-enforcement to intervene. Then you end up going to trial, practically emptying your account and some family members', too. My aunt and my mother did that, all while Cain held onto the key piece of information that would have meant that money—and me—would have stayed where we belonged."

Rahm adjusted the sleeves on his tailored white shirt as he stood. "All the while knowing you weren't the guilty person, but all of these things were still happening. The one word to describe what I felt the moment those prison doors closed behind me was—devastated."

He stood, gripped the back of the chair in an attempt to stay in a peaceful vibe, using those techniques that Chaz Maharaj, the Knight of Bronzeville, had taught him. "Never in a million years did I think I'd be in that situation. But it took me a couple of years to get over the fact that this reality was my new life. Actually, my mother, Aunt Alyssa, and my ex—whenever she found the time—kept me connected to the outside world."

"Your brother," Sheikh Kamran said. "That was a betrayal of the worst kind."

Rahm looked him straight in the face. "You asking me or telling me?"

Sheikh Kamran glanced at Jai, but it was Rahm who said, "I'm being sarcastic."

"Oh, sometimes American sarcasm can be a little hard to follow," Sheikh Kamran admitted with a chuckle. "My beloved is giving me a major lesson in that." He leaned in to whisper. "Do not tell her I failed today."

"Word," Rahm said, holding out his fist for a pound.

Sheikh Kamran obliged, touching his fist to Rahm's.

"Oh, so you know what this is," Rahm teased.

"My wife's class reunion was what brought her here," Sheikh Kamran said with a smile. "Trust me. I can give some *dap* or a *pound* properly."

The three of them shared a laugh, then he added, "And we will work on the licensing and placement for the tattoo shop. Just give me a little time, all right? In the interim, I will cover your employees, their housing, and medical care until we have things sorted out.

Rahm nodded, feeling somewhat relieved. "Okay. I'm going to trust you on that."

"Speaking of your brother," Jai patted Rahm's shoulder. "You need to discuss your mother's situation with Shaz soon."

Rahm said, "I'll do that." He released his breath, knowing he was going be leaving Durabia on the same day as his aunt. He had to bring his mother here and hoped that his aunt made that decision as well. The weight of Marilyn's decision settled on his shoulders, along with all the other implications that wouldn't work in his favor.

# Chapter 8

Alyssa observed the busy waitstaff as they tended to the patrons who sat on the terrace of the B'Stilla Cafe, enjoying breakfast entrees that were a blend of American and Middle Eastern cultures. While she waited for her nephew to finish yet another meeting, she'd write a few chapters. She believed he was going to be late, so she might as well use the time well. She pulled out her yellow, blue-lined tablet and settled in.

A few minutes later, she looked up, and Rahm stood at the table looking down at her.

"Look at you, arriving all early and whatnot. Five whole minutes to spare." She laughed and placed her pad back in her bag.

He greeted her with an embrace and a kiss on the cheek. "I see you got jokes this morning,"

"What's wrong with your face? You have to change that, nephew. Your expression is so sour it seems like the first time I changed your diaper." She laughed so hard the couple at the table next to them looked at them with amusement and also laughed.

"See, why you want to bring up old stuff." Rahm couldn't help but chuckle. "I'm a little pissed this morning. Marilyn isn't coming to Durabia."

He took a few minutes to catch her up on things.

"Don't worry about Marilyn right now. She's what, fifteen years older than you? You need a woman who can give me some grands to spoil. Have you looked at the gorgeous women over here?"

"Age doesn't matter to me." Rahm picked up his menu. "I don't get down like that. I love this woman unconditionally, no holds barred. She is my present and my future. I just need her to see that." He signaled for the waitress. "Let's order. I promised you breakfast."

"Oh, so you remember that now, huh?"

"See, there you go again," he teased, scanning the restaurant. "The B'Stilla Café, Auntie? Really? Did you choose it because it sounds like a place where you're going to get your groove back?"

"First of all, it's B'stilla, not B'Stella. They named it for a Moroccan pastry. Second, that would have to take place in Jamaica, nephew," she corrected with a laugh. "Third, I don't need you speculating about *my groove* or anything else south of *my border*. Thank you very much."

After placing their orders, they made their way to the buffet, spread with a vast selection of fresh fruit, cold and hot cereal, juices, and small breakfast quiche that would serve as appetizers until their main meal came. Rahm glanced around the restaurant and noticed all the families present; the businessmen who were combining meetings and breakfast. And the women closer to his age; as pretty as they were, none of them held a candle to the love of his life.

"Enough about my relationship troubles, have you decided if you're staying?" Rahm asked while they tasted their selections.

Alyssa inhaled deeply, as if that action alone would satisfy her hunger. Once seated, the rich scent of the fresh pastry on her plate was calling her name. "Honestly, it's beautiful and all, but I haven't been here long enough to really make a choice." She lowered her gaze to the table and then back to her nephew. "It does bear consideration, though. When I was at work, and human resources made me feel that because of my age, I had no other options but to tolerate my boss's blatant disrespect, I was devastated. A woman of a certain age never wants to be without possibilities. Marilyn may be feeling this as well. We don't like to feel trapped."

Rahm touched her hand. "Auntie, why didn't you tell me that happened to you?"

"You were on probation, and I didn't want to be the cause of your return to that place." She patted his hand before breaking off a small piece of the pastry. "Now that I'm here, I've noticed the same societal strife that we deal with in the United States. I don't want to trade one environment for the other. At least when I'm home, I know what to expect."

She lathered on several pats of butter.

"Gee, Auntie," Rahm said, pausing mid-bite. "You aren't worried about cholesterol or anything like that?"

"Hush. If I'm going to be bad, I want to be real good at being bad."

The arrival of the servers silenced them. After the waitress delivered their meals and ensured they had everything they needed, she moved to the next table.

"At least here you have someone on the throne who cares about all people. Sheikh Kamran is not concerned with his own selfish ideology. He has a heart for the people and wants to see them prosper."

She poured syrup over her cinnamon swirl pancakes while Rahm asked, "If money was no object, and you could do anything you desired, what would it be?"

While waiting for her response, he tasted the spinach omelet he ordered.

"I really want to try my hand at having a successful writing career. I've put some novels out there, but they haven't hit higher than the national bestsellers list. Mostly because I didn't have the bandwidth to put into marketing and promotion like I should. The day job took up way too much of my time," she admitted, angered that she'd given so much energy to people who in the long run didn't appreciate it. "If that doesn't work, I can teach classes on writing. I know all of the formulas and could help newbies break into the industry." Alyssa cut a piece of those fluffy confections while she spoke. When she put the morsel in her mouth, she released a moan.

Three men at surrounding tables turned to watch the woman who released that erotic sound.

"Auntie, please don't do that here," Rahm said, glaring at the men.

Alyssa scanned the men's faces, but what arrested her attention was the envy in the eyes of the women who sat at those tables. "My apologies, but this is delicious."

"I can introduce you to Sheikha Ellena, Amanda, and all the other Black women who have started a new life in Durabia. We can put our heads together and find something for you to do that will give you some stability. Since you won't let me take care of you for all that you did for me."

She placed her hand over his. "That's what family does."

"You mean *some* family," he teased.

"I don't get your meaning."

"Some family. If that had been Cain—"

"His ass would still be inside. Old knucklehead Negro," she said around a mouthful. "Next time I see him I want to give him an old school pop upside his onion head."

She turned over her coffee mug, picked up the green tea bag, and before she could drop it into the cup, the waitress appeared and poured hot water.

"Thank you," Alyssa said as the waitress scurried away to attend to other customers. "I am fine with meeting with those women you mentioned. First, I have to decide if I want to stay."

"That's fair. Just keep me in the loop. I feel all of my plans are falling apart. Now that Marilyn's not coming, I have to go home and get my mother before anything happens to her."

Alyssa paused with the fork midway to her mouth. "What are you talking about? Why did you say before anything happens? Nothing is going to happen to her. She's in a secure facility. Calm yourself, nephew."

Rahm parted his lips to say something then clamped shut. Almost as if he wanted to share something but thought better of it.

They finished breakfast, then caught up on family news and avoided the question she so clearly wanted to ask. He paid the check and stepped outside where the heat of the Durabian sun flowed over them.

"You have more grown-up plans tonight?" Rahm asked as he guided her near the valet parking area.

"Here ... here's what happened ..." she sputtered when she saw who stepped out of a Mansory Vivere Bugatti.

Rahm nodded toward the familiar figure walking their way, "Oh, I see what you been into, Auntie."

"Stay out of grown folks' business, and it's not what you think," she said out of the corner of her mouth.

Ahmad extended his hand to Rahm. "Hi, you must be the nephew. I'm Ahmad Maharaj."

Before he returned the gesture, Rahm studied him for a moment. "Rahm Fosten. Nice to finally meet the person who has kept my aunt occupied since she arrived."

"Your aunt has been very helpful in teaching my son, Taj, to read. He is quite smitten with her."

"You don't say," Rahm said, and his tone was skeptical as he handed over a business card and waited for Ahmad to do the same."

"All right, enough with the introductions," Alyssa said, stepping between to the two men. "Taj will be waiting for us."

Rahm wrapped his arms around her, and she hugged him back. "See you later, Auntie, and be careful."

"I'm in good hands, baby." She released a throaty chuckle. "Very good hands."

She walked toward the vehicle with Ahmad who touched her elbow, and sent an unexpected jolt of desire up her spine.

# Chapter 9

"Miss Alyssa," an excited Taj screamed as they crossed the threshold of the house. "You came back." He wrapped his tiny arms around her waist. "Morning, Father," he greeted Ahmad, who didn't seem surprised by his son's reaction to a woman who they'd just met the day before.

"Yes, Taj, I'm here. We have another story to write today," she responded, waiting on his response for his new favorite activity.

He pumped his little fist in the air. "Awesome."

"Good Morning, Taj," Ahmad said, playfully ruffling his son's hair. "So Miss Alyssa is the only one who gets that reaction from you."

Lauren, who had stood by watching Taj's excitement, said, "He's been bouncing with enthusiasm waiting to show you what he read earlier." She gently pulled him away. "Let's allow Miss Alyssa some time to get situated, and then she can begin your lesson."

"Okay, Mother," Taj replied as he hurried over to the family room.

"Ahmad, would you get us some herbal tea, please? I want to chat with Alyssa for a few minutes," Lauren said, touching Alyssa's elbow guiding her to a tinted glass-enclosed solarium.

"Sure," Ahmad said, and headed toward the kitchen.

Alyssa placed her tote on the empty chair at the entrance and joined Lauren at the patio table. "How are you feeling today?"

"Today is one of the good days," Lauren replied, looking out on the pool that was surrounded by an array of cabanas that provided protection from the sun. "How about you? I know this assignment with Taj was not your reason for being in Durabia."

"I'm doing well. I had breakfast with my nephew this morning." She glanced over her shoulder following the sounds near the entrance. "It was great catching up with him. We'll meet up again later."

Ahmad entered, carrying the tea set and placed it on the table along with some honey and sugar. "Enjoy, I'll be with Taj until you're ready for him."

"Thank you," they responded simultaneously to his retreating frame.

"We're taking time from you enjoying your visit with him," Lauren said, continuing the conversation while pouring them both a cup of tea.

"My plans were to write, get in a little shopping, and enjoy some of the sites to make a decision on living here permanently. Then I met your wonderful son in the park." She reached for the raw sugar, adding some to her tea. "Plans changed a little, but it has been my pleasure to help Taj. He's a delightful boy. How old is he? Seven or eight?"

"I appreciate you saying so. I tend to think he's a joy as well, but what mother doesn't think that of her child?" She winked and her lips turned up in a smile. "He's nine actually, but a little small for his age compared to some of his classmates. His father started that way, then sprouted in the teen years." She dripped a little honey into her tea. "Where are you from originally?"

Alyssa returned her cup to the saucer. "I'm from Grand Crossing, on the South Side of Chicago." She scanned the spacious solarium that extended from a kitchen any woman would die for. "Do you live here?"

"No, Ahmad recently settled here, then wanted me to come, hoping one of the brilliant doctors at the symposium could find a cure for my illness."

Lauren and Alyssa both smiled as they overheard Ahmad tell Taj, "Good job".

"I was born in D.C., but met Ahmad in California where we both went to school. We were there until I filed for divorce because he deserves to be happy and not tied down to a dying wife ..." She paused as though gauging Alyssa's response.

If Lauren didn't volunteer the reason, Alyssa had the presence of mind not to pry.

"You seem to be enjoying Ahmad's company."

Alyssa's eyes shot up from her cup. "Oh, it's nothing like that. I think he has designated himself my personal protector." She finished the last of her tea and refilled the cup.

"Trust me, it is exactly 'like that'," Lauren countered. "He's as smitten with you as our son. I'm happy to see him showing interest in someone worthy of his time."

"There is Susan," Alyssa replied, over the top of her steaming cup, knowing all this talk of being smitten was much too soon.

"No, there is not," she said through her teeth and her green eyes flashed fire. "Ahmad is honorable, even to disrespectful women like her," Lauren explained. "But I want to know how you feel about him?"

"He seems like a great father and a great provider," she said, locking a gaze on Lauren, wondering what her game was. "I can tell that he still cares deeply for you."

Lauren smiled, nodding. "Those are some of his qualities, yes, but you carefully skirted answering my question, hoping I didn't notice."

"Oh, you're very perceptive; we'll get along great." Alyssa's soft laugh brought on Lauren's as well. "He is attractive, any woman would find him as such." Her smile faded, and her voice took on a serious tone. "But I'm not that woman who would upset a happy home."

"Honey, please, we are not a happy home," Lauren replied, crooking her fingers like quotes. "This is co-parenting at its finest, and that is all there is. Nothing more." She gestured toward the family room. "I'll let you get to your lessons because I know Taj is anxious."

# Chapter 10

"Permission to hold you?"

After their second night at the Bliss event, Alyssa was more comfortable with Ahmad. Now she was more than half sleep, as it took him an hour to get up the courage to ask since he brought her to his home. He had never feared rejection before. The word wasn't even in his vocabulary. But he wasn't certain how this enchanting woman would receive him—not like this. All of the rules ran through his mind, and he realized they were essential to her. He wanted to extend that sense of comfort and safety as they grew familiar with each other.

Her answer was a long time coming, and it wasn't much of one.

Alyssa cleared the fog, gave him a stern look before her one-word reply came. "Why?"

"Because I interrupted the experience for you tonight," he answered, leaning on the arm of the white sofa.

"It's fine," she said, adjusting the pillow. "We're still at the milder events. They're preparing to take things to the next level tomorrow."

"You didn't answer my question." The lights were dimmer now. In the stillness, the creaks of the house settling carried to Ahmad. Several couples had ventured past the holding stage. Maybe *they* had some history, but he needed to move slow with Alyssa if he made any moves at all. Enjoyed having her with him tonight.

"No, I didn't," she countered, and her lips lifted in a small smile. "It isn't necessary that you make up for lost moments because our conversations monopolize most of the encounter."

"It is for me," Ahmad said, noting the time on the clock across the room, he realized that at this hour, she should be in her hotel, not here with him. Having her walk into her hotel after such a late night amounted to more than a "Walk of Shame" here in the Middle East. He did not want that for her.

Lauren and Taj were fast asleep, and Susan was in the upper level suite.

"Then my answer is ..." She paused, looking at the pool through the open door, her eyes reflecting the lights shimmering from the water while weighing her options.

The irritation that filled him was profound, and he almost, *almost* disregarded the protocol he learned earlier tonight for how these sessions were supposed to be conducted. Permission was ultra-important to her for some reason. And he understood boundaries better than most. He'd lived within them all of his life.

His mother, Talsa, was forced to leave India after his father had been embroiled in yet a second international scandal. The first involved a prominent and well-known place in India that people all over the world visited—The Taj Mahal.

*His father, Preekesh Maharaj, was the unfortunate beneficiary of the Taj Mahal Corridor Project when a former government counsel related to the project accused one of Ahmad's family members of pocketing a great deal of the money. She had purchased properties for herself and some of her loved ones and was then brought up on charges of corruption and embezzlement. Talsa had warned her husband not to partake in any of the bounties.*

*If this scandal had happened with any other building, everything would have remained under the radar, but the length of time it took to get things done, pushed the issue to the forefront. Political inference had caused the Supreme Court of India to also cite the slow progress in coming up with answers about where and how those millions had disappeared.*

*With all the infighting the project became obsolete, and new plans were made to remove the partial construction near the Taj Mahal site and instead replace it with a green landscape and flowers.*

*Such lofty ideas derailed by greed. Preekesh Maharaj lost everything and had driven the family into abject poverty. Unfortunately, he did not learn from this mistake and fell prey to yet a second scandal—the fake housing loan, which was uncovered by the Central Bureau of Investigation in India. He didn't listen to his wife, for yet the second time. Because of the media scrutiny, government investigations, and the embarrassment brought on by his greed, Talsa had to pack up Ahmad and his brother, Jameel, late one night and travel to Durabia, then plead for the forgiveness of the family she left behind when she married one of the East Indian Maharaj's instead of a Durabian Khan, as had been arranged..*

*Talsa made sure specific values were implanted in her sons. She pushed them towards excellence, which was why Ahmad became a surgeon and years later, landed at Durabia's top medical center and a private medical practice with Silverstone Clinic that focused on Homeopathy. He found that people made it through surgery just fine, but it was the aftercare that sometimes killed them.*

This week, Ahmad made sure he had only a limited role in the world medical conference that his practice sponsored. He also took time off from his surgical rotation to spend with his dying ex-wife and son, hoping one of those doctors would look at Lauren's chart and history and come up with some type of treatment that would prolong her life.

Still, his new medical partner, Susan, had somehow horned in on the experience and one of the other partners asked about working more closely with her on her aspects of the presentation—the same one had asked Ahmad to host Susan in his lavish home since she was single and his wife wasn't too comfortable after meeting her. That should have been his tip off. He believed in the best of people, and he saw the best until his family arrived, and the entire dynamic changed as though someone had flipped a switch and turned on the "ugly" in Susan.

Ahmad regretted saying yes, within moments after the word left his mouth. Susan may be everything a man would look for in a partner— successful, charismatic, and intelligent, but she was not what he needed in a relationship or as a mother to his son. Children and pets were an excellent gauge of character. Taj disliked her from day one, and Taj liked everyone. If they still had Tiger, their Golden Retriever, he would probably feel the same way. Unfortunately, they had to give the family dog away to someone else when he displayed the same illness and symptoms as Lauren.

Alyssa Porter was fast becoming a woman who occupied his thoughts and had brought peace into his life. And now he waited for the permission that would allow him to share an intimate but non-sexual moment that would connect them in some small, but meaningful way.

"I guess it would be all right," she said in a voice just above a whisper. "It's not sex or anything like that, so ..."

Maybe it wasn't the *'hell yes'* he desired, but it was consent, all the same.

Ahmad slid next to her, wrapping his body around hers—the "big spoon". She stiffened at first, but slowly relaxed into him—the "little spoon".

Grateful wasn't even the word. He'd been fending off females at the event all night. For some reason, he only wanted this woman right here. One who did not seem impressed by his money or status. A woman who would rather embrace strangers than him.

The soft even breathing signaled she had fallen asleep. Ahmad caught the flicker of a shadow at the door and Susan's shocked expression. She retreated from the doorway, but not before he caught the malice in her eyes as she glared at them.

He made a mental note to contact the partner who had planted Susan in his home and shift her either to a hotel or the partner's home, because staying with Ahmad was now out of the question.

Every man that came near Alyssa tonight, quickly picked up that she was off-limits. Even he didn't understand this sudden possessiveness when it came to her. The thought of another man with his arms about her disturbed him for no reason he could explain.

He might have succeeded in fending them off tonight, but what the hell did Bliss Level 3 entail tomorrow?

# Chapter 11

"I've got good news and bad news," Shaz said, seated behind his desk. His office was situated on the fourth floor of the building Sheikh Kamran owned. His Brother King's head office was on the upper floors, but he preferred to be closer to the ground, where a few flights of stairs could have him outside and into the warmth of the sun.

*The building was a construct of Sheikh Kamran's father after he listened to a young Crown Prince who asked, "We started a fishing and pearl diving economy. Then China took over that industry, and we almost failed to recover. So, we shifted to oil like so many countries in this region. What happens when solar energy becomes a new way of life?"*

*Aayan, the ruling Sheikh at that time had asked Kamran. "Oil is what our world and economy are built on, what would you have us do?"*

*The young Crown Prince replied, "We should become the best in everything. Technology. Medicine. Culture. We change how the world sees us. Everyone should want to come here and enjoy the beauty that Durabia has to offer."*

*Slowly, the kingdom made efforts to shift from an oil-based economy to a hospitality and tourism focus. Then with its emphasis on technology, medicine, and bringing their history and architecture to the forefront, Durabia gained international acclaim.*

Standing two steps inside the door, Rahm snapped at his lawyer, "Good news or bad news? How?"

He'd become tight with Shastra Bostwick since he accepted the coveted position of being a Knight of the Castle. Nine kings in total were united to solve the assassination attempt on their mentor's life. With formidable enemies such as The Russian Mafia, crime lords, dirty politicians, crooked cops, and shady business executives, they used their professional skills to render justice their way and return The Castle to its original humanitarian purpose.

Then Jai expanded Khalil Germaine's vision by putting the concept of the Knights of the Castle on the table. These men would be mentored by all of the Kings, who would also guide them into becoming businessmen and leaders in their community. Eventually, they would also mentor other enterprising young men.

"I've had an interesting forty-eight hours, and at this point, if one more person hits me with the wrong thing, I'm ready to shoot first and ask questions never." Rahm glared at the loc-wearing, Jamaican man as he took a seat across from him at the desk.

Shaz inhaled as if taking that all in, then used Alyssa's classic line, "So, what had happened was …"

"Aw, come on, don't start with that bullshit."

"Your brother …"

Rahm tensed on hearing those two words. The anger remained at what Cain had done, merely because of jealousy, the desire to obtain Rahm's material possessions, and the need to tap into his loved ones. Rahm had his suspicions that his ex, Brittany, had been with Cain during his incarceration. Her guilt might have been the reason for the lack of communication.

"He now has power of attorney for your mother—medical and property. His lawyer messengered a copy to the office," Shaz continued, sliding the sheets of paper toward him.

Rahm didn't say anything for several minutes as he read the document. Then he blurted, "What in the entire hell?"

The papers he held informed him that his mother couldn't come to live with him in Durabia without permission from the one man he knew wouldn't give it. "What happened to the one we put in place?"

"I pressed you to designate someone to take over those responsibilities if something happens to you, but you never did. You were still vacillating over whether that should be your brother, and it was never completed or signed by your mother. I told you time and time again, Illinois does not allow a POA without delegates."

Rahm ran a hand through his short-cropped hair. "And what does this mean for the lawsuit you just won? And the disability issue with the Social Security people?"

After he sorted a handful of papers, Shaz said, "Your mother is about to come into a large sum of money due to the settlement with the insurance company. And she's going to receive a lump sum from the back pay in the disability case, but it might be disputed because of the settlement. There's a bigger issue if Cain empties her bank accounts. She won't be able to qualify for disability because of this money that came through for her."

"Then she'll be at my brother's mercy." Rahm gripped the edge of the desk as he stood, trying not to take his frustration out on the one person who had been in his corner besides the other Kings and his aunt. "How did he even get her signature on that paper?"

"He went by the facility because Marilyn permitted him to gather your mother's things for the trip to Durabia. That's when he had her sign the POA."

Rahm sighed into his hands and stood straight. His mother couldn't possibly know what she had signed. And Marilyn couldn't see the damage she'd done. Not only was she leaving him, but in passing off the responsibility of traveling with his mother, she also allowed a world of hurt of another kind to enter Rahm's life.

Before he left to start the businesses and get everything settled in Durabia, he moved his mother to a facility for patients who suffered from dementia. For as long as possible, Rahm had kept his mother, Lorraine, in the six-flat where she'd lived all her adult life. But it became increasingly difficult to keep her safe. At one point, he had a house phone installed because she kept losing every cell he bought her.

Now, at the facility where he'd placed her, Lorraine "believed" she worked there and that the director was her supervisor. She mentally stressed herself about other people's issues but didn't have anything to do.

Cain having power of attorney meant the least responsible one in the family now controlled her well-being and finances. And since his mother signed the document, Rahm couldn't fight it, and truthfully, he'd been tired of constantly going up against his brother. In fact, if Cain saw to their mother's needs, Rahm wouldn't have a problem. But he already knew how this situation would end. Cain would blow through that money so fast, it would be like it never existed. Then his mother would be vulnerable to elder abuse. His brother did not handle frustration well. And their mother could be a handful. Not because she wanted to, it was the nature of the disease. Patience was the key. Chaz Maharaj had been a godsend and taught Rahm so many calming techniques. Cain had no such coping techniques.

When Rahm was first released from Menard, he was required to stay with his brother because his mother had been hospitalized. Somehow, his brother had slid right into the upscale co-op Rahm owned on the north side of Chicago. Had also taken over his accounts, his clothes, his tattoo equipment and anything else that belong to Rahm. Those were the worst three months of his life. At one point, Cain could've put Rahm in jeopardy by saying the wrong thing while he was still on parole. Cain was well aware of the power he held and often used it to his advantage. Tried to get a rise out of Rahm by strongly hinting that he'd slept with Brittany.

Brittany had denied that accusation all the way down the line.

Shaz rounded the desk and sat on the edge in front of Rahm, interrupting his mental agony. "Vikkas and I are working diligently to resolve this."

Rahm could believe that, but it was too late and felt like a whole new betrayal. "None of what I experienced before compares to the knife that my brother consistently sinks in my back. Every possible turn he tries to undermine what I do, but this is a new low, even for him."

"Sometimes family can be your worst enemies," Shaz replied.

As if Shaz knew anything about that. His brothers had careers that meant they didn't have to resort to the type of things Cain did to get ahead. Then the bonus of the Kings meant Shaz had an army of intelligent, resourceful, and powerful men to rely on when things went South. Rahm had only recently become a part of this venture and wasn't sure how much he could ask in return.

Inhaling a calming breath, Rahm said, "You don't know how much I'd like to believe he's going to do right by my mother. I already know if money wasn't involved, he wouldn't be touching this in any shape, form, or fashion."

He shook his head, fighting despair. First, his professional life imploded. Then his intimate relationship went sideways.

Now, this.

*Dippin' is coming for you.*

Rahm had to figure out how to navigate this new round of madness and get his mother out of America when he had no legal standing to do so.

# Chapter 12

"I don't want her here," Susan said, slamming the manila folder on the kitchen table where Ahmad had set up shop while Alyssa worked with Taj.

He looked up from the document he held. "That's not your call to make. She is my guest and Taj's. You've you're only in my home at John's insistence because of the mishap with your residence."

And that had been the worst thing that he'd given in to. John explained the lay of the land and how married men were seen as more stable and reliable. Single men made others uncomfortable, even given the two to one spread of men to women in the city. John had dropped Susan into the mix, claiming that he felt more comfortable having her in a residence while he secured one that met with her stringent requirements. Whatever that meant.

"This week was supposed to be about us and our brand. Not Lauren and Taj, and definitely not her," Susan said.

"You don't get it." He pointed between the two of them. "We are strictly business partners."

"What is it with you and her?" Susan whined. "And where did you go last night?"

The memories flooded his mind and almost brought on a smile.

"That information will remain confidential."

"Now you're keeping secrets," she accused.

"No, I'm keeping her confidence," Ahmad countered.

Susan's flushed skin displayed her real emotions. "You don't know her well enough for that."

Her attitude was annoying, and he did nothing about the sting in his words when he responded, "And you don't know enough to say anything on the matter."

She stood in front of the table, both hands propped on her waist. "Well, the fact that you were all wrapped up last night says a whole lot."

Lauren walked into the room, glaring at Susan as she said, "Please keep your voices down. I can hear you in the family room." She turned to leave, but not before catching the death glare Susan sent her way.

"Nothing more than that happened," he replied. "Not that it's any of your business."

Her eyebrow quirked upward, and she zeroed in on him again. "But you wanted it to be more?"

Surprisingly, he did, but no reason existed to share that information. He needed to analyze his feelings when it came to Alyssa. Was it merely the lack of intimacy that made her so intriguing?

Since his divorce years ago, he had chosen to remain celibate. Only later did Lauren accept him into her bed for comfort, not necessarily for sex. He had to wonder was it also the fact that his ex was pushing him in Alyssa's direction and blocking the hell out of Susan?

When he first witnessed her tears while they were at the park, he, too, was drawn to her, wanting to find out the source of her pain; what had disturbed her soul. The moment Taj reached out to her, eliciting such a warm smile, he was … smitten. *Yes, that's the word.*

Her kindness and patience with his son were so touching. And for her to open him up to the very subject that gave him the most challenging time was a blessing. When he asked how he could repay her, and she answered, "You can't, and I wouldn't ask you to," his heart somersaulted. Surely, everyone could use money.

That's when he decided to find out what she had to gain, based on their exchanges. How could he know what she wanted unless he understood what she had chosen to experience while in Durabia?

She said he could never repay her. He wanted to show her how wrong she was. Everyone wanted something. Everyone needed something. At least, that's what he realized in his culture—everyone had a price.

"Either she goes, or I do," Susan said, smirking. "You see, there are so many benefits set to come to you and the practice based on *our* partnership. It would be a shame if you missed out because you prefer slumming with the help."

Ahmad stiffened at the ultimatum. He weighed his choices. She brought a lot—professionally—to the table, but that's all he needed to consider. He could already tell an entanglement with her would turn dark and messy. Their businesses were newly intertwined since she had breezed into the country and used top-level connections to secure a partnership with the private affiliates he had been in business with for several years.

She came highly recommended, even if she had been a little aggressive, almost as if she had something to prove. Upon learning of his marital status or lack thereof, she had begun taking things to a totally different level and seemed frustrated that he didn't fall in line with whatever her designs on him happened to be. One of the partners had been trying to get Ahmad married off to every single eligible bachelorette in his entire family. He had failed, so now Susan had been the latest of tributes.

He gave her his full attention. "I'm not going to dignify your presumptuousness with a response. I'll see you at the office. Have a great rest of your day."

Ahmad left her fuming and headed for the family room. Let her ponder his lack of response to her threats.

The moment he stepped into the room, a smile settled on his lips. His son was reading a book that he'd picked up in a quaint bookstore near the Durabia Mall.

As Taj pointed to a picture on the page and Alyssa watched, Ahmad was grateful. The excitement his son displayed reached all the way into his soul. Only a special kind of woman could inspire this, the same way his mother instilled in him a desire to succeed past his father's failures. Not because she wanted them to live down his mistakes, but she wanted them to live up to their full potential.

They had trouble locating that program Alyssa mentioned so she used construction paper and flash cards to recreate it. Improvisation. Resourceful.

"You don't know how beautiful that is," he said, keeping his focus on Taj as he stopped next to Alyssa where they sat near the patio doors.

She raised her head, locking a steady gaze on him. "What?"

"Seeing him excited about reading, and he's writing, too."

"He's a brilliant child," she said, smiling with such warmth and sincerity he could have embraced her.

"I'm glad to hear you say that," Ahmad replied, as Taj marked the place where he was reading and closed the book. "Let's go to the market for some breakfast. I'm famished."

"I think I'll pass." She gathered her things as Susan came around the corner. "I'm going back to my hotel suite," Alyssa said. "I've spent so much time here that I don't know what it looks like."

Taj's excited expression deflated. "You won't have breakfast with us, Miss Alyssa?"

"I'm sure your father would love to spend some time alone with you."

"Dad, can we do that alone time another time? Because right now, I'd like some Miss Alyssa time."

*Yes, I would like some Alyssa time too.*

"That's fine. Miss Alyssa needs to eat, too. Her stomach was growling."

She gasped, then protested, "It was not."

"Uh-huh," Taj teased, giggling. "Then what do you call this …" He made a sound like a Mack Truck.

Ahmad roared with laughter, and Alyssa turned an intense shade of crimson.

"Fine," she mumbled. "Breakfast, and then I leave."

Taj went to her, embraced her warmly and would not let go.

Strangely enough, he never did that with anyone, especially Susan. And it had never before crossed Ahmad's mind that there might be trouble on that score. Somehow since his family came to Durabia, things were a lot clearer. Susan could not keep up that façade.

Susan seemed to tolerate Taj, but she didn't have a welcoming personality, which was the main reason he made sure Lauren was present at all times when Taj was out of his sight and Susan was around. He still took care of her despite the fact they had divorced long ago. The divorce freed him to be with other women, but his love for Lauren remained. She was still his wife in every way that mattered—except the sexual sense; something that angered Susan to no end. It was not Laurens's fault that she was dying. But it was his choice not to abandon her.

His commitment, despite laws and paperwork, meant he would be with her until her dying day. On the hardest of nights, he lay next to her as the pain wracked her body. Here it was, he was a top surgeon with access to a world of resources and none of them had been able to help his wife. *Ex-wife*! He had never felt so helpless in his entire life.

Even though they lived separately in the States, he always provided anything she needed to make her life easier. If Susan had her way, Lauren would not be with him at all, though he had been honest about the arrangement and the fact that it wouldn't change. Lauren had initiated the divorce because he refused to go that route. She wanted him to be free to live his life without the burden of her illness.

He never saw it that way. He continued to love and care for her, although he was not legally required to do so. Morally and legally were two separate things, but he was content to provide for the woman who had joined her life with his and given him a son.

When Susan entered his life, after one of the managing partners helped her buy a way in with a substantial investment and American connections, Ahmad saw the benefits of joining forces since their interest and business savvy were at the same level. He should have left it at business with no chance for it to become something else. Allowing her to edge into any kind of social relationship had proven problematic.

Even more so, when Taj seemed more of an irritant than the bonus a child should be to a woman who didn't have any children. Now he understood. She wanted all the benefits, but none of the responsibilities.

The fact that Taj gravitated to Alyssa so readily, and Lauren also seemed secure in their interactions, said everything. Never had there been a time when she felt comfortable leaving Taj alone with Susan. Now that he saw the exact opposite with Alyssa, he would put some distance on every aspect of their relationship—including business. His child was an extension of him. If Susan couldn't accept Taj after all this time, she never would.

"Where do you think you're going?" Ahmad demanded when Susan whipped out a tube of red lipstick and touched up her pouty mouth and a sinking feeling hit the pit of his belly. And the partners would have to get over his single status. *It is what it is.*

"I'm going to breakfast with you."

"No," Taj said, and that one-word command echoed the length of the house. "I want my Dad and Alyssa. My mother can go, but I want to enjoy it."

Susan flinched and glared at Taj, who seemed to wither for a second. Then he gripped Alyssa's hand and looked to his father for reassurance and assistance.

"We'll see you later," Ahmad said, leveling a stony gaze on Susan, a warning for her to stay in place.

"When is she leaving?" She asked, ignoring Alyssa. "Her presence disrupts this household."

"She is not," Taj said, tightening his hold on Alyssa's hand causing her to look at him.

"Only when she's ready," Ahmad confirmed, picking up his son's queues, moving past her. "And contrary to what you believe, this," he spread both arms out, "is *my* household."

"Right," she snapped at his retreating back. "As long as she knows her place in it."

Ahmad whirled to face her. "What the hell did you just say?"

"You heard me," she shot back with the boldness of a tigress. "I already have to share you with Lauren. I don't relish the thought of sharing you with someone else. Otherwise, I might have to walk away from the business end of things. And you know John and the others will not want that."

Alyssa stiffened, parted her lips to protest and set matters straight while the grooves in the record were still being cut, but he held up a hand to bring silence.

"First of all, you do not get to dictate who has what place here," he said in a tone that barely concealed his anger. "Didn't you give me an ultimatum before, and I chose her?"

Alyssa's soothing tone cut through the tension. "Taj, let's wait in the front room."

"'Kay," he said, looking up and smiling at Alyssa.

But they both froze a second later, as Taj refused to budge no matter how much Alyssa tried to pull him away.

"Second, you are a guest," Ahmad's words transfixed all of them. "No matter how you try to frame our relationship or push it in the direction that you want it to go. Lauren isn't going anywhere. Neither is my son. You consider both to be an inconvenience, and I have turned a blind eye, hoping it was simply a phase because you feel empowered since you're backed by the founder of the International Business Council. But, no matter what he planned, things are not going to work. Not only are we on different pages, you're also not even turning ones from the same book." Ahmad rolled up his sleeves. "We are going to breakfast, feel free to make good on your threat to leave. It'll do us all a favor."

"You're not choosing her for her," she snarled, circling him. "You want her because of your precious son. Everything is always about him. Even Lauren's presence here is all about your pleasing a child, who you indulge more than you should."

Ahmad left the doorway and came back toward the center of the parlor. "Let you tell the story, my son shouldn't be given any consideration whatsoever. I'm doing what's best for my son. Taj, and Lauren, will *always* be my first consideration."

"Come on, Taj, we shouldn't be here for this, I—"

Ahmad gave Alyssa a warning glance, and she clamped down on anything else she had to say. His attention returned to Susan, who he pinned with an intense stare. Without looking at Alyssa, he said, "Take him with you. I'll be right down. See if you're able to snag us a seat near the waterfall."

Alyssa quickly ushered Taj through the door and down the hallway.

# Chapter 13

Rahm stifled his impatience but couldn't help the sting in his words. "You just had to do an end-run around the process, didn't you?"

"She's my mother, too," Cain protested, the smug sound of his voice let Rahm know that his brother was grinning on the other end of the line.

While pacing the floor of his living room, Rahm threw a cursory glance at the paperwork Shaz had given him. "She's been your mother all this time, and you haven't done squat. So why all the sudden interest right now?"

"Maybe I'm just being mature," he taunted. "Trying to be like you and e'rethang."

"And maybe you're just trying to get your hands on that money she has coming?"

"Aren't you?"

Rahm scanned the area of his home, some of it draped in construction plastic to protect the furniture and all else. Now he had this huge residence, and it looked as though no one would be living in it. Not his mother. Not his aunt. Not the love of his life.

"No," he replied to his brother. "The difference between us is that I don't need her money. I have my own."

"Well, some of us got it like that, but I don't. And the difference between you and me is that I have actual time to take care of her. You're out here running off to Pakistan somewhere and leaving her with random folks."

"It's Durabia. The Middle East," he corrected. "And she wasn't with random folks. She is in a private, luxury assisted living facility that I paid for. So, she was doing fine." Rahm gritted his teeth to avoid yelling.

"Well, once this month is out, I'm rolling her up out of that place, and she'll be in my crib."

Rahm slumped to the floor, forgoing the chairs—the effect his brother always seemed to have on him. Now, he planned to take their mother to that level, too? "Your one bedroom?"

"That's what I got, so ..."

"And where is Mama going to sleep?" Rahm asked, watching his housekeeper answer the door.

"On the couch," he replied. "It's a pull-out. Queen size."

Rahm wanted to reach through the phone and strangle the man. "Did you ever consider that she's a woman, and in need of private space?" Rahm came to his feet when the housekeeper ushered Aunt Alyssa inside, and he embraced her.

"She's old," Cain snapped. "She doesn't need that much space, or any privacy."

Rahm dropped the phone on the sofa, trying to gather his bearings. His mother had sacrificed everything for both of them to have what they needed, even when she was in lack. She'd been the one wearing run down shoes while they had brand new ones. She had left several relationships with men she loved, the moment they showed any sign of mistreating her boys. Mostly, they were irritated at the extra baggage her boys presented in the relationship. She put them first. Always. Was it too much to ask for them to do the same?

Evidently, Cain didn't get that memo.

"What's going on, number one nephew?" Alyssa asked.

He picked up the phone, put it on mute and answered, "Cain now has mom's Power of Attorney. It's not by coincidence that it happened now when I'm out of the country and can't fight it. The timing is perfect, with her settlement payments beginning in the next month. He has no consideration for her. This is about him."

The look Alyssa gave him would've made a lesser man cringe or suck his thumb.

Alyssa snatched the phone from Rahm and put it on speakerphone. "Cain."

"Auntie, so he took you with him too?"

She continued to hold Rahm in her peripheral. "No one takes me anywhere. I go where I want. Let's talk about you. What the hell are you doing, Cain?"

"I have no idea what you mean, Auntie. I'm just trying to ball like my brother."

They both gawked at Cain's laughter that sounded like a mix between a hyena and a clown.

Rahm handed Alyssa something to drink as they both moved to the patio to have a seat. The scenic view and the breeze from the river would help them deal with the stench from the piles of manure his brother was shoveling out.

"The only problem with that is, I'm balling on my own dime, and my efforts," Rahm said through his teeth.

"Well, I'm doing it on my efforts as well," Cain said with resentment coloring his voice. "Mom and I will be fine. Maybe we'll get a two-bedroom, later. You and Auntie can stay over there. You always were her favorite anyway."

Alyssa sat her glass on the patio table before she spoke, "What you're doing is going to come back and bite you in the ass. It is shallow to take from those who have tried to help you all your life. Your mother raised you better than the way you're behaving. It's time to grow up and stop doing dumb stuff. Be a man. For the record ..." Her gaze locked on Rahm, "I never had favorites. You were just always wallowing in shit. At least your brother cleaned his up."

# Chapter 14

The view of the city was beautiful from Lauren's bedroom. The pearl grey colors in the room were warm and blended with a pop of navy-blue. Tranquil blue waters and green palm trees greeted Lauren outside the sliding glass door. From one end of the balcony, she had a perfect view of the sea and city, while from the other, the patio and gorgeous swimming pool shimmering below.

Now, she perched on the edge of the bed, focused on her ex-husband who sat near the doorway. "I totally approve of Alyssa." She wore the widest smile Ahmad had seen on her in a while. "She's a beautiful, compassionate woman. She is articulate, witty, and has a fast tongue. She will make you a good wife."

"You don't count," Susan snapped from the couch, glowering at her.

"And that's where you're wrong," Ahmad countered, passing Lauren a glass of water to take her meds. "Her opinion matters a great deal. It seems like when I don't listen to her is when I run into problems."

Susan had found her way back into his home again using the International Business Council and John Freeman, the owner as a buffer. He saw right through the ploy but couldn't very well make a scene in front of John, who had somehow failed to secure the type of the housing Susan required, or an alternative as Ahmad had requested. The hotels were full because of the medical conference, or so he said. When he left, she had stayed behind under the guise of having a business discussion with Ahmad. That's when Lauren saw fit to go for the jugular.

Lauren swallowed the pills and drank from the glass. "The fact that you are in his life hovering around like a vulture is the main reason I'm still fighting to stay alive. I don't trust you with Taj. Never have. I don't trust you for Ahmad. I can't even die in peace."

Ahmad stood, his glare bouncing between the women. "What are you talking about?"

"I'm so ready to go," Lauren whispered, gripping the edge of the bed. "The pain never goes away. It greets me in the morning, and it says goodnight before I fall asleep. I am tired, Ahmad. I am ready to go home." She inclined her head toward Susan. "But I can't leave you and Taj, not with this woman trying to make her way into your life as your intimate partner."

"You bitter, clingy bitch," Susan growled and those blue eyes flashed with anger. "His partners already know what's best for him and their business. And you don't have to worry about your precious son, that's what boarding schools are for."

"That's it, I've had enough," Ahmad roared. "I'm packing your things. You are a guest and you disrespect my child, the mother of my child, and even a guest who came to my home."

"No, I have this," Lauren said, focusing on Susan. "Go on, speak your peace."

"You've always wanted me out of the picture even though he's set to make more money than he's ever made in his life since I came to the practice."

"I wouldn't give you the satisfaction of dying," Lauren spat. "As long as you're breathing and have access to my son, I will fight." She shook her fist in the air. "Even from the grave, I will make sure you're not the woman he ends up with. You only want Ahmad because he makes you look good overall—in business and on his arm. Plain Jane from a little town in Mississippi. The new age power couple."

Lauren uttered the words with such disdain that it caused a spike of guilt to stab Ahmad's heart. He had never seen this side of his wife. *Ex,* he reminded himself. *Ex-wife*.

"And he's going to help you exit stage left," Lauren said through her teeth. "I'm sure there's an Air Bitch & Bitch where he can park you and that broom you flew in on."

While it was true that several lucrative contracts helped him reach multi-millionaire status, the partnership agreement with Susan brought nearly seven times his worth. The reach of his healing techniques and medical practice expanded, but would come at a cost: Lauren's happiness and his son's.

He trusted his ex a lot more than he trusted a woman who managed to obscure certain aspects of her past and finagle her way into a high-level position simply because his business partners only saw dollar signs— and lots of them. And they kept mentioning that they would feel more comfortable if he was a settled, married man. A single man—rooster—in the henhouse that made up the female population of Durabia, presented problems. At least in their estimation.

Despite Susan protests, he'd requested a more thorough background check and couldn't wait to receive the details. Why had she landed on Durabia's shores, if she held such influence and power in America? Why did it seem she was trying to wheedle him down the aisle in order to finalize the rest of the contracts she had dangled in front of the other investors associated with her? If he married a second time, he wanted the marriage to be as wonderful as the one he had with Lauren.

*Ahmad and Lauren had married after they obtains their bachelor's degrees. He had a stint in medical school, and things would be tight for a while, especially given the fact that his family's finances were still deficient because of his father's actions. All of his schooling had come through scholarships and grants, and he made sure he kept the kind of grades that would bring in more opportunities.*

*She worked as a librarian until she became pregnant with Taj. When he finally started doing well, they decided she could stay home. Life was good until he started traveling more, and she became seriously ill. Then Lauren divorced him to free him from watching her die, but also to find love again with someone who would take care of the two men in her life.*

*That hadn't happened so far, and they'd been together for years beyond her diagnosis.*

"I am going down to join Alyssa and Taj for breakfast. Would you like to come?" he asked, standing and moving to the bed.

"No, I'm going to rest," Lauren said, placing a hand on his chest.

"Are you sure?" He took one of her hands in his.

"I'll be fine," Lauren whispered with a flick of her wrist, shooing him from her bed. "I thank you for always looking out for me." With that, she rested her head on the pillow as Ahmad left the room with Susan trailing him.

"But first," he said over his shoulder. "I will pack Susan's things to make good on her recurring threat and my own. Air Bitch & Bitch. That's a good one."

Mere inches on the other side of the door, Susan pleaded, "We can work through this."

"No, we cannot," he said, marching up the stairs to her room and filling her suitcases with her belongings.

"I will do better with Taj," she said, her tone a lot less fiery than it had been, as she sank down on the bed near him. "I promise."

Ahmad had put some distance between them with his long strides, but turned to face her, "You cannot fake what is in your heart. You have already shown me everything I need to know, and that I was unwilling to accept. How can a woman claim to be so enlightened, yet, so vindictive, resentful, and malicious?"

He dialed his partner's number, counting the rings in his head, "John," he called out when the familiar voice came on the line. "Look, this partnership with Susan is not going to work. I don't care what your reasonings are or your end game is. Not only did she insult Lauren, but she disrespected my child and another guest in my home. Somehow, I managed to make arrangements for her somewhere else." He inhaled sharply. "So, I don't want her to have to lug all of the stuff, but I'm not spending another second in close proximity to someone this toxic. Come and get her."

John's reply was simply, "I understand, that is why she couldn't stay in my house. We wanted what she could bring to the organization, but it's not worth your family's stability."

Ahmad snapped the bags closed and slammed the last drawer closed. "I was hoping you would understand." He headed down the stairs carrying the first of many of her designer bags and set them at the door. Susan ran behind him trying to keep up.

"To be honest, I'm surprised you lasted this long. I'm on my way."

Ahmad disconnected the call, then turned his focus to Susan, "I have secured you some other lodging so you can finish out the rest of the sessions for the conference, but the partnership aspect of things is finished. I don't give a damn how much money you have. We have money."

"But I have things you don't have."

"Don't care about your connections, either. We'll do just fine."

She twisted her hand to lace their fingers. "People like us and accepted us together," she said as her tears flowed.

"They will adjust." He slid his cell into his pocket. "Change is part of life."

She wiped her cheek with a delicate gesture. "How can you be so cold, unfeeling?"

"Me? Cold? Boarding school? Die already? Are you seriously accusing me of that?" His gaze narrowed on her. "You meticulously followed my career, then targeted the partners in my private practice group, found a way for a mutual friend to suggest doing those first workshops and then tried—really tried—to pull something more by having your friends intervene from day one. The calculation involved in that kind of planning was master level." He stepped closer, putting his mouth to her ear, "But it ends today. John's on his way. He planted you here, it's only right he do the honors—"

"All because of that bi—"

"Class act, Susan. Real class act."

Ahmad brushed past her and headed down the stairs to get her up and out. Taj, Alyssa, and breakfast were waiting.

# *Chapter 15*

"Why did you contact my brother?" Rahm asked Marilyn, trying to keep his voice level.

"I didn't have anyone else who was willing to go to the Middle East."

He moved to sit at the kitchen table where his dinner waited. The staff had prepared his meal and retreated.

"Right," he continued, "but to ease your conscience, you did it without discussing it with me first. Now, I have legal problems because Cain's not willing to come to the Middle East to bring her, either. He's aiming to empty her bank accounts, and you gave him the avenue to do just that."

Marilyn sounded stricken as she asked, "What do you mean?"

"He pulled a fast one. Had her sign a Power of Attorney that puts him in control of everything."

She gasped, but he didn't give her a moment to reply. "Now, my mother won't be coming here to be with me, where I can take care of her properly. He's going to move her into that little dump of an apartment and put her on the couch. Thanks, Marilyn. Thanks a lot."

"Rahm, I'm so sorry," she whispered. "I didn't know."

In between bites of couscous and vegetables, he said, "That's the point, you contacted someone you have no relationship with to step in and do *your* part. It'd be different if you would have at least brought her, then turned around and went back."

"But you would have convinced me to stay."

That stopped him for a second, then he regrouped. "No, you would've stayed because I'm good for you, and to you. Because you want to be here and that is not ego talking, baby. Those are the facts."

*Early on, Marilyn had fought to stay with him, and they had kept their relationship private from their respective families because their love was so new. Then their first test arrived. Rahm woke up from a sound sleep dreaming he was making love to Marilyn, only to catch a glimpse of some strange, half-naked woman running from his bedroom.*

*Rahm backtracked to the previous night and knew he wasn't drunk. Nor was he the type of man to cheat on the woman he loved. The cathedral windows let in the brilliant sunlight to set the stage for this drama that was unfolding. Marilyn and the naked woman faced off. All he could do was plead, "I didn't touch her."*

*From the look on his love's face, she needed a little more convincing. "I don't know who she is." The naked woman turned out to be Marilyn's youngest daughter. Then to make things worse, another woman burst through the door, calling her 'mom' as well.*

*How bad could things get? This little scenario was supposed to be enough for Marilyn to exit his life and continue to allow her ex to dictate her existence. Thanks to the newcomer, they would soon find out that her ex was behind the whole scam. Crystal went on to tell how their father promised money to Wanda, the naked one, if she managed to seduce Rahm. Amazingly, that little heifer still didn't see anything wrong with her actions because she just stood there, butt naked as the day of her birth, with her arms folded under what was clearly a pair of costly, surgically-enhanced boobs.*

*"Apparently, he's upset that you moved on." Crystal stated, while giving Rahm a thorough once-over.*

*Marilyn quickly schooled her daughters about what was going* on. *"It's not that he wants me back; it's because he loves seeing me unhappy."*

*With a little prodding, the youngest finally decided to share her side. "I needed the money. Besides, you wouldn't help me, so I helped myself."*

*At this point, Rahm wondered how long Marilyn's ex would have an impact on their relationship. He was willing to help her and fight for her, but she had to want out. If the man was willing to use his own flesh and blood in this manner, what else had he used her for? Was Marilyn even thinking about those implications?*

*Wanda thought she was grown enough to seduce a real man, yet she wasn't woman enough to handle her life without her father's money.*

*"He hasn't loved me from day one, yet he used you to break up my new relationship just because you can't figure out your life," Marilyn said. "How selfish of you."*

*Marilyn apologized for her doubt, but given the situation, he would've doubted himself.*

*"And tell your daddy you failed," Marilyn said, causing Wanda to pause mid-step. "Failed, at trying to destroy the best thing that's happened to me since I gave birth to both of you. Failed, at trying to take this little slice of happiness from me." Then she wiped away a tear with the back of a trembling hand. "Let's see how your daddy will take that."*

Now here they were, back to having issues. He thought that since he threw Victor out of his house on another occasion where he made the mistake of putting his hands on Marilyn, this kind of doubt and upheaval were behind them. Apparently, that wasn't enough. He was still a part of her life, and her daughters had more say over what she did than Rahm realized.

He finished on a small portion of his meal and placed the plate in the fridge. "I would not force you to stay," he whispered, knowing she was right about the convincing part. "Big difference. Convincing allows me to state my case. Forcing means I don't give you a choice. And I already know what that's been like, not having a choice." He adjusted his earpiece before continuing, "But bringing my brother in behind my back, that's some next level pain you're putting on me right now. You knew what he did that took six years of my life."

"But I didn't think you would want her to go with a total stranger," Marilyn countered.

"True, but I didn't think you'd pair her up with my enemy."

"He's her son," she said, raising her voice. "It's time he stepped up and did the right thing."

"And that wasn't for you to decide." He picked up a polo shirt and pulled it over his head, "She's *my* mother. I was responsibile for her and was doing all right."

"So, all right means that you didn't secure that Power of Attorney like you were supposed to," Marilyn shot back. "Yes, I made a mistake, but so did you. You can be angry at me, but the person I think you really should be angry with is yourself. None of this would be an issue if you handled your business."

Rahm walked back into his living room, switching over to the handset. "Marilyn, I'm going to hang up before I say something we'll both regret. First, you break my heart by telling me at the last possible minute you've changed your mind about us and our plans for the rest of our lives. Then you involve someone who has no idea what it's like to care for someone other than himself and then consider the outcome a mistake." Rahm stared at his phone wanting to toss it across the room. Instead, he took in several calming breaths. "Right, so it's all me. I get it. Goodnight, Marilyn."

# Chapter 16

Prince had made this particular action that took extra time between lovers popular. Usher had also made a specific type that left lipstick on the leg even more popular.

A kiss was harmless, right? A quick one—press of lips to lips—was purely topical in nature. Then why was Ahmad feeling some kind of way about experiencing one with Alyssa Porter?

"You were saying?" her voice snapped him to the present as they maneuvered the hallway to reach the second floor of the condo for the Bliss Level 3 event.

"Never mind."

She paused, peering at him. "What did you do?"

Ahmad formed the most innocent face he could manage. She gave him the evil eye, and he responded with a sheepish grin. "Do you want me to leave?"

"I didn't ask you to come," she replied, picking up the pace again. "You came on your own. I still don't understand why."

"I made a judgment about what you planned to do, and I only wanted to know what this is before I make another mistake."

She glanced at him over her shoulder. "Why do you even care?"

"I'm not sure."

"Oh, you're sure," she taunted, and her smile was one that didn't quite reach her eyes. "You just don't want to say it out loud."

"I need … I want … I just …"

Alyssa gave a low throaty chuckle that unnerved him.

Embarrassed that she could know him so well, he admitted, "Yes, I do know. With what you're doing for my son, how can I repay you? I think I can do so by learning what it is you need and becoming exactly that. Am I right?"

The vulnerability he felt at that moment was profound. What made it worse was that she could read him and his intentions with accuracy.

"I don't need you to do anything for me," she said, splaying a hand across his chest. "You shouldn't take that personal."

"Would you like … never mind," he said, against his better judgment. "I'll leave."

When the conversation they had the previous night flowed through his mind, he froze, wondering if he was about to make another mistake.

*"I attended two or three Big Spoon-Little Spoon parties,"* she said. *"And then they invited me to a Bliss event. There are levels to this. And I skipped from Level 1 back in the States to a Level 4 party, thinking I'm a big bad woman, right? I soon found out that I was not that grown. The event was nothing short of an organized orgy,"* she said with a laugh. *"Now that was some grown folks' stuff, and I was the only Black woman there. And I have to tell you that you white people are into some freaky shit."*

*"I'm not White,"* Ahmad said over the rim of his wine glass.

*She gave him a sidelong glance. "Close enough."*

*"I think I should be offended by that."*

*"Well, facts, shaking the family tree, and all that,"* she said, chuckling. *"So, I went to the party, you know, for research purposes for my books and everything."*

*"Right, research,"* he said in a skeptical tone.

*"I'm sitting on the couch with my clothes on and my popcorn. They said watching is participating, so I watched my ass off. I'm looking sideways, upside down, different shapes, different sizes, ass everywhere.*

*I saw some toys there, too. But they happened to be on the opposite end of a chainsaw. Dildo on one end, and when they turned that bad boy on—"*

*"You got up and left?"*

*Her beautiful lips curved into the widest smile as she said, "No, I was more like 'honey, I'm home'."*

*Nothing short of an organized orgy.* And she expected him to leave her in this place.

They secured a seat at one end of the spacious living area, and Ahmad shared another anecdote. The minute he extracted himself from her and stood, another male with blonde hair and blue eyes—handsome in a college prep sort of way—took his spot. The man's gaze flickered over Alyssa's lush curves, and he was almost drooling.

"Permission to kiss you."

"No," Ahmad said without a moment's hesitation. Then froze when he realized his error. He had actually spoken his thoughts out loud.

The blonde's expression went dark. So did Alyssa's.

She glared at Ahmad, then said, "I thought you were leaving?"

Ahmad took in the predatory vibe of the man sitting next to Alyssa. "Not without you," he answered in a firm tone.

"I have a way home," she replied.

"I'm not leaving without you," he insisted.

"Then stay and watch," she snapped before returning her attention to the guy sitting with her.

Several people abandoned their conversations and had taken an interest in the exchange.

"So, about that kiss," the blonde hedged, sliding to close the distance.

"No," she repeated while putting her focus back on Ahmad.

He couldn't hide his relief even if he wanted to. Why did leaving her in this den of men bother him so? He could have any woman he wanted—even those who swore up and down they preferred someone who looked like the man sitting next to her at the moment.

The minute his divorce became public knowledge, women from all walks of life somehow found him to their liking. When it came to encounters with women, it had been a long while since he'd been off balance the way he was now.

She shooed the man away and looked up at Ahmad, who reclaimed the space next to her.

Alyssa was a refreshing change. Her sensuality simmered just under the surface. She seemed totally unaware of her effect on men and women alike. Here, in this environment, everyone was fully attuned to the contradictions warring inside her—the tense body movements when someone came too close, the uncertainty about what she wanted to experience, and the doubt that came right after her decision. The men in this place had picked up on the one thing he had already figured out from the first time she spoke of her lost love—that unbridled passion was waiting to be unleashed from the depths of her soul. The man on the receiving end of it would have an experience he would never forget.

Alyssa missed Tony—the intimacy, the love, the belonging. Her need to be "claimed" by a loving mate was all too prevalent, even in "sort of" embracing this kind of experience. He wanted to be that man. The need to be "that man" was overriding every ounce of common sense.

Even here, in this safe space, he didn't dare leave her to someone else. Alyssa was his. She didn't realize it, even though everyone else was slowly coming to that understanding.

"Permission to kiss you," he whispered, leaning closer.

When had he ever uttered those words to a woman? He always knew. Always. But now he waited, wanting that yes. Uncertainty filling him, not knowing what her answer would be. Curious gazes galloped their way, as others wanted to follow any developments—since no one last night and now, could get close. To her or him.

"Yes."

He reached for her, guiding her from the sofa, drawing her close. His lips were on hers, teasing, tasting, arousing. Ahmad felt Alyssa's complete submission.

As she moaned, he held on and deepened their connection through her moist mouth. Her sighs were all the guidance and direction he needed.

Someone whispered, "Sweet Jesus."

"No shit," someone else responded.

Ahmad didn't stop. Couldn't if he wanted. All eyes were on them as she responded with a passion he knew she was capable of, and her reaction brought on a different type of thrill.

He reluctantly broke away to gaze into her eyes so filled with heat, it took every ounce of control not to splay her on that sofa and take her to what he considered would be Bliss Level 5, right then and there.

She settled down, laid her head in his lap, and curled up like it was the safest place in the world. Several men watched the exchange, and Ahmad didn't miss the jealousy in their eyes. The blue-eyed man lurked, watching Alyssa. The hairs on the back of Ahmad's neck put him on alert where this man was concerned. He would make sure she was never alone with him in these surroundings.

"I'm not leaving without you," he whispered against her ear several hours later.

Alyssa sat up and laid eyes on the blonde-haired man, who lingered in their vicinity. She grabbed Ahmad's arm, and they were downstairs and out the door in the next moment.

They barely made it through her bedroom door thirty minutes later before he realized he still needed one more thing.

She sat on the end of the mattress and crossed one leg over the other. The split in her dress allowed a pleasurable view of her thighs.

"Permission to kiss you again?"

Alyssa smiled a little, seeming to enjoy his discomfort.

"That's how it works, yes?"

Her smile widened. "Yes, that's *exactly* how it works."

"I didn't want to—"

She stood, and her lips were on his in seconds.

The kiss carried them to the bed and lasted for what seemed an eternity. They ended the night spooned and connected.

Ahmad had never felt such peace. He hoped she felt the same and that their connection would lead to something even more special.

# Chapter 17

Rahm balled his fist so tight his knuckles paled. "Jai, I don't understand her. We made plans for *everyone* to move. That's why I had the construction crews stop working so the architects could redesign the house. That way Mom, Aunt Alyssa, and Marilyn would have massive master bedroom suites of their own so they would feel like queens. She was on board with everything. Then at the last minute, she decides she's not coming and tosses my mother to the big bad wolf." He paced the length of the office with Jai watching every move.

"Calm down, brother," Jai said in a patient tone. "Sometimes women can be caught up in things in your presence, and yes, it all sounds good. Then when they're alone, and reality sets in, or people get in their ear, things aren't as clear as they thought. Give her some time. She is level-headed. She will figure it out."

Rahm held his peace but reflected on the first day Marilyn made her presence known. Maybe Jai did have a point when it came to Marilyn expressing her true feelings. It wasn't as if it hadn't happened before.

*"You came here, to my place, for a reason," Rahm had said to Marilyn Spears several months ago when she showed up at his home unexpectedly. "We could've had this conversation at my job, or a café somewhere, right? What's really going on?"*

*Marilyn sank into the cushions of his sofa and folded her French*

*manicured hands on her lap. The act alone made her seem small,*
*vulnerable, and beautiful. "Not for what I have to tell you."*

*Rahm leaned against the door jamb for a few moments, then he*
*moved away, closed the door, and waited.*

*"The latest audits and investigations need to be taken up to a Senate*
*oversight committee to put an end to them once and for all. Mr. Maharaj*
*needs to figure out why Donald Amos is gunning for him, or he will lose*
*everything. It seems personal."*

*With both arms folded across his chest, Rahm said, "You're not*
*supposed to tell me that."*

*"No, I shouldn't do any of this. But my conscience won't let me*
*sleep." She nodded slowly. "I've read up on Mr. Maharaj, and I like*
*what he's trying to accomplish."*

"Okay, I get that. Thank you. I'll find a way to help him." Rahm
grinned, then crossed the distance between them. "But since that's out
of the way … why are you really here?"

Her gaze locked on his. She slid off the sofa and made her way to the
door and swung it inward. Defeat shadowed every step.

"So that's how it is, huh?" He shrugged as she looked over her
shoulder. "Just come all up in my joint, side-step the real issue, and walk
out like I'm not supposed to know something's up."

She blinked twice, and he witnessed the war going on within as her
expression went from fearful to total confusion.

Rahm moved forward, placing a hand on the door to close it, but still
kept a three-inch space between them. Her eyes were so beautiful in their
hazel-green glory. A flicker of desire lit in them that was so fleeting he
wasn't sure it had been there. Then her lips quivered and parted slightly.
An invitation? Maybe? Wanting to say something? Maybe that, too.

"Tell me what you want," he whispered.

"I don't know."

"Oh, you know all right," he teased, resisting the urge to pull her to
him and let her feel exactly what he wanted. "You're just afraid to say
it."

She didn't respond.

Rahm moved away to take a seat on his tattoo bench. "Why don't I sit right here until you find the courage to get to the point you need to make." He frowned. "I'm not going to make it easy. Your being here says a whole lot, but to be sure I'm not overstepping any unspoken boundaries, you have to say something else."

"I ... I ... shouldn't." She shook her head. "You know, this was a mistake."

Frowning, he said, "This what?"

"Coming here."

"Okay. So, you came to tell me that Jai's business is in danger from the people you work for. I already knew that. What else do you need me to know?"

She swallowed hard, her body trembled a little, and the heavy warmth of arousal fueled his next action. He was with her, pressing a kiss to the softest lips he'd ever touched. "Talk to me," he whispered into her hair. "Speak what you want me to know." He trailed his tongue along the fullest part of her lips, and she whispered his name.

The sound, both a plea and a prayer, was his undoing. He held on to his sanity long enough to say, "You have to tell me what you want."

A tear slipped from the far corner of her eye as she tilted her head back and looked directly into his eyes. "I want to know what love feels like."

That sobered him. All thoughts of making this woman lose her absolute mind went out of the window.

"I want to know that I am worthy and needed, and ... loved."

Marilyn was asking for much more than physical gratification. She wanted more from him than any woman had ever asked. For her to be this open, this vulnerable, meant everything to him. Rahm pulled her into the wall of his chest, trying to calm the storm he felt was rising within her. "Let me see how we can make that happen. Are you down for that?"

*"Yes." Her breathy one-word answer was all the confirmation he needed.*

*That night, he devoted himself to adoring and pleasing Marilyn, leaving her in no doubt that he desired her. Since then, he'd done everything to make her dreams resemble what she wanted to be her reality.*

*"So, how does this work?" Rahm asked after they made love. "I work for the man your department is investigating. The wrong move, I might add, but still. Does make for interesting dinner conversations, though."*

*"We keep work out of this," Marilyn answered, splaying a hand on his chest. "The investigation is going to be over as soon as the patient has the child and the police gather what they need. And if Mr. Maharaj can uncover Donald's hand in this or he waits for the evidence that will prove you all are innocent; everything will be fine."*

Infamous last words. *Everything will be fine.*

Jai called his name, pulling Rahm from his memories and back to the current moment. Once again, he asked, "Rahm, are you good?"

"Yeah, I am," Rahm said, breathing out hard. "I apologize for coming here like a hothead. This, and the situation with my mother, has me so frustrated I feel I might blow a gasket."

In a few steps, Jai crossed the tiled floor to reach Rahm. "Trust in the love the two of you share. Continue with your plans. Everything will work out."

Jai's hand on his shoulder didn't help Rahm control his disquiet. With one last look at his friend and mentor, he said, "If this has anything to with her ex, there will be hell to pay."

# Chapter 18

"His background checks out." Charli, the hostess gave a nod of satisfaction.

"Background?" Alyssa asked as they stood at the entrance of the tri-level condo where the event was being held.

"Yes, when he signed up for Bliss 4 and 5 at the last minute." Charli sighed at her puzzled look. "We had to vet him. He purchased a full week pass to be in compliance, and one male dropped out, so it makes our numbers even."

A woman who Ahmad recognized as one who was in hot pursuit of him two days before, scolded the fiery hostess, "But he turned his nose up at the idea."

Charli tossed a hand in the air before she responded, "A lot of people do until they understand what this really entails."

"I didn't mean to bring trouble," Ahmad stated, trying to squash the twenty questions before it created a scene.

"No trouble at all. We needed to weed out the bad seed. Background checks can only cover so much. It can't tell us who's an asshole or a whole ass," Charli replied, but her comment was directed at the man walking her way.

Oliver, with blonde hair, grey eyes, and a face pretty enough to grace a woman, gestured to Ahmad. "Well, he has violated three times. He was late the first day, added to the registry at the last minute; then, he didn't ask permission on several occasions when it came to her. And don't give me that bullshit that they're paired up. She admitted she didn't know him much longer than us."

Alyssa noticed his roaming eyes raking over her body and stepped within Ahmad's reach.

"You've given him special treatment for the very same thing you've had others escorted out for." He moved closer to Alyssa. "If you're going to be fair, you have to do it across the board."

"That's right," Stewart, a dark-haired jock type, chimed in.

Ahmad studied the faces glaring at him, and didn't want to cause Charli further embarrassment. "Thank you for allowing me this time. I will leave you to it. Good night, Charli. Goodnight, everyone." He put his focus on Alyssa for a moment. "I'll be waiting outside whenever you're done. Take your time."

Alyssa was right behind him.

"Where are you going?" Oliver followed her, almost sounding alarmed.

"If he's not welcome, then neither am I," Alyssa replied, walking to the door. "I broke the rules a few times myself. So …"

"Wait," Stewart said, getting to his feet from the post he had taken on the arm of the chair, "Let's talk about this …"

"You can't have it both ways." Charli glared at the man, and he inched back.

Alyssa replied with one foot out the door, "He goes. I go. Goodnight, Charli. Thank you for everything."

"Call me," she said as she rushed forward to embrace Alyssa. "I want to know how this all works out. And I want an invite to the wedding."

"He's already married."

"Is he?" Charli flinched and narrowed her gaze on Ahmad. "Something tells me you need to look into that."

Stewart walked to the door and spoke from behind Charli. "Maybe we can overlook it this one time, I mean."

"Would you feel the same if I told you that there's a one hundred percent chance that none of you will get a 'yes' from me?" Alyssa locked gazes with him over Charli's shoulder.

Oliver winced.

"I was honest from the beginning. In the Opening Circle, I said, hope I can spend some time with a gorgeous Black woman." Gabe, a buff guy with spiked hair, gave Alyssa a once-over.

Alyssa stiffened, and she glanced in Charli's direction with no indication whatsoever that she would consent to that.

"Is she actually here to play or just watch?" he growled when no answer seemed forthcoming.

Ahmad shrugged and said, "Ask her."

"I'm here to ..." she trailed off, blinking as she mulled over her answer and only came up with, "I'll see."

Oliver maneuvered past the table, chaise, and sofa and stood near the door. "Are you just teasing us?"

Alyssa frowned and took a step farther into the room. "What do you mean?"

She didn't miss the fact that Ahmad didn't leave her side.

Oliver licked his lips and motioned toward her. "All of this lusciousness, and you're keeping it to yourself."

"None of the rules say I have to do anything," Alyssa argued, drawing the attention of other couples in the room.

*Pajamas stay on at all times. You don't have to physically interact with anyone. If you mean yes, say yes. If you mean no, say no, and if you mean maybe, say no. You can always change your mind later.*

Gabe ran a thick hand through his well-styled hair. "No, it's just that several of us would like to ..." He flickered a gaze to Ahmad, who simply looked at him, waiting.

"I just hope there is one night when you leave him at home," Stewart added in a gruff tone.

"I didn't bring him," Alyssa countered, placing a hand on her bosom. "He came on his own."

Gabe's head tilted; a spark of lust lit in his eyes. "So, you're not an actual couple?"

"No, we're not," she replied, ignoring Ahmad's warning glare. "I told you all before; I met him only hours before I met you."

Oliver did a double take, thought that over, then a grin split his ivory face. One that matched Gabe's and Stewart's expression, as well.

"Sounds good." Oliver bypassed Ahmad and stood face to face with Alyssa, smiling as he asked, "Permission to touch you?"

"No," she snapped.

All eyes arrowed in on her.

His smile disappeared and the grimace that followed spoke volumes. "I don't understand you."

"You don't have to." She moved past him to plant herself on what seemed to be her special place on the sofa. "You seem to believe that my *presence* here represents consent. It does not. Evidently, no one has ever told you 'no' before. Might want to get used to it here. A major part of the lesson is accepting 'no' gracefully."

Gabe stormed away but tossed an ugly parting look over his shoulder.

Ahmad moved in and sat next to her, studying her face. "Are you all right?"

She turned her head toward the door. "Don't speak to me right now. You're doing this deliberately."

"What?" he said, affecting an innocent grin. "I don't know what you mean."

"Bullshit." She stared him down for a few minutes before he said, "Goodnight. I'll wait for you outside."

"You don't have to."

Ahmad stood and held out his hand for her, "Then come with me. I want to see you safely home," he offered.

She placed her hand in his and stood inches away, but he leaned toward her. He caught himself and inhaled as he found his bearings.

Alyssa, not worrying about the rules or anyone who was still watching them, met him the rest of the way to complete the kiss.

"He didn't ask permission," Stewart mumbled, motioning for Charli.

They pulled apart as both glared at him.

"Everyone plays by the rules—even him," Gabe chimed in, gesturing to Ahmad.

After Ahmad was out the door, Alyssa stared at the vacant space next to her wondering why she wasn't more persistent in asking him to stay.

"Now, where were we?" Stewart gave her a grin that sent a shiver of unease down her spine.

"We weren't anywhere, and it's going to be a 'no' for you each and every time."

Was it her skin tone? The fact that she was the only one of her kind there? Her hair, her body type? What was drawing them? And why didn't any of them appeal to her? The thought of kissing Ahmad again aroused her more than she wanted to admit. Her panties didn't know whether they wanted to stay up or down.

Charli held out Alyssa's pink shawl. "Go to him before you start a riot up in this place."

"I don't understand," Alyssa replied.

"Woman, you are so in heat and don't even realize it," she warned. "The only man you want is him—be honest with yourself."

"I don't even know him."

"You want him," she insisted. "Fulfill that need and get to know him better later. We're grown-ups. We can do stuff ass-backward."

Alyssa glanced toward the door, "I'll admit that I'm a little turned on by him, but that doesn't mean I'm ready for sex."

"Go. Be with him. Tomorrow come prepared to play, even if it's just a little, and it's only with him." She ushered Alyssa to the door, then leaned in to whisper. "We love it. The more unfulfilled they are, the better they are with us. Some of us already know Bliss 5 is going to be off the charts."

Alyssa choked back her reply.

"Stay in control," Charli warned. "Make him follow the rules. You'll thank me for it."

"But we're not here," Alyssa protested. "That only applies in this setting."

"The rules apply wherever you need them. Ahmad knows them and the reason they exist." Charli tossed over her shoulder. "Use them."

# Chapter 19

"Promise me you'll take care of my son and my husband."

Alyssa looked up at Ahmad, then down at the pale, fragile hands that clasped her own. She didn't know quite what to say to Lauren who insisted on this and put Alyssa in this awkward position. What she was asking was more than anyone should at this stage of the game. "I will do my best, but this is sudden. I mean, I didn't even ask or anything like that."

Lauren nodded, signaling for Ahmad to leave them. He complied but still seemed worried.

Alyssa perched on the side of the bed.

"Didn't you ask God to send you a placeholder until the real number came along?" Lauren asked with a wan smile. "So Tony was the placeholder, and Ahmad is the real thing."

*In retrospect, Tony wasn't a placeholder. He was the one who held my dreams; the one who had my heart.* "I stopped asking for much of anything after he was killed that weekend when there was a rash of violence throughout Chicago," Alyssa replied. "I learned the lesson. I'm still learning that lesson. I have too much emotional baggage to bring into a relationship. That's why I never sought to have another one."

"But the prayer was still out there in the Universe," Lauren countered, adjusting on the bed. "Did you think God would forget?"

Alyssa laughed. "So, you think Ahmad is the answer to my prayers."

"Isn't he?" Lauren questioned. "It seems to me he has every quality you listed in those intentions you told me about."

Damn, the woman was right about that. He did. Every single one. But he wasn't hers to have, his heart belonged to Lauren. And Susan wanted his ass to belong to her, too.

Alyssa glanced down at her pedicured feet. "I'm feeling different about me. I don't ... I just live, you know. Make sure I look presentable. Now I'm second-guessing my clothing choices. Put perfume on more than just my wrists."

"He's bringing out the seductress in you."

Alyssa frowned as she glared at Lauren. "I don't like it. I've never been so aware of myself. Except with ..."

"Tony." Lauren smiled as she heard Taj's laughter with his father in the family room of the house.

"I used to think about him every day," Alyssa confessed. "I haven't even thought ... Not since, Ahmad—"

"Well, there is that," Lauren said. "Just go with the flow and see where it leads."

Alyssa fanned her cheeks with a hand as she returned Lauren's smile, "Are you certain that—"

"I'm sure," she answered. "I've co-existed with this for years, and I just want to go peacefully. But I couldn't do that with Susan gunning to become his wife. I mean not just a girlfriend or lover, but a wife. And she said it outright, and I don't understand why she was trying to rope him into marriage so fast. I just felt something evil from her, despite her outward appearance. At first, I thought it might be jealousy tainting my view, but watching her with Taj let me know for sure. She would harm him just to have Ahmad all to herself."

Alyssa had wondered about the state of his relationship with Susan, but more so, if he was aware that she didn't like children.

"What kind of person would harm an innocent child just to have a man?" Alyssa asked.

"The kind of woman who's been after him since the moment she landed in Durabia. He deflected everything until some of his partners in the private practice became involved."

Alyssa opened her mouth to speak but thought better of it. She loved that Lauren treated her as a friend and didn't want to overstep and meddle in their marriage. Non-marriage.

"Susan was all over him. So hard, that he had the organizers put him on a flight right after the initial negotiations ended, instead of extending it for the few days they requested."

Alyssa didn't quite know what to say to this. She had her own reasons for not liking Susan, but none of it mattered. At the beginning of next week, she would be leaving Durabia, and Ahmad Maharaj would be a thing of the past.

"I never liked her," Lauren said, taking a sip of the water Alyssa offered. "Professional doesn't mean entitled. She fails to realize that the Creator gives what purely belongs to you. You don't have to steal it. You don't have to force it. You don't have to pretend to be someone other than yourself. She never seemed to embrace that."

Alyssa learned a long time ago that the good Lord would only give you what you asked for, with a few surprises thrown in if you weren't specific.

"You're asking me to do something so important for Ahmad and Taj," Alyssa said, replacing the glass on the bedside table. "And you barely know me."

"I know a good person when I feel it," she said. "Ahmad is a good man. I had no choice but to divorce him. He was hurt, but he would not have tried to move on if I hadn't let him go."

Alyssa kept a watchful eye on Lauren as she laid her head back on the pillow before saying, "And if you really think about it, he still didn't let me go. We've been living in the same house. He sees that I get the best care. I travel when I'm able."

Slowly Lauren shifted to a more comfortable position. "They don't make men like him anymore. It irks Susan to no end that he still refers to me as his wife."

"To be honest," Alyssa said with a smile. "It was kind of confusing to me until you explained it."

"I normally tell people it's an open marriage so there are no misunderstandings. Then they'll understand that he can pursue any women he's interested in." Again, she patted Alyssa's hand. "He hasn't shown any interest in anyone. That is, until you."

"He doesn't know me."

"Our son does," she said in a voice just above a whisper. "Pure heart. Those tears brought him to you. Your quest to find yourself compelled my husband." Her smile lit up her face. "My beloved. He has never been with Susan physically, and that pains her entire soul. And on some level, it pleases me that he wants you more than he ever wanted her." She held up a hand to stop Alyssa's protest.

"Before I became this ill, he would come to me first, and I did whatever my body would allow. It has never been enough, but he would rather have the little I can give than to accept anything from her."

Alyssa could only listen, surprised at the level of information that was being shared. In the back of her mind, there may have been questions of residual feelings between the two of them.

Lauren leaned forward and, with an expressive sigh, said, "You have my blessing."

She repeated her words, taking Alyssa's hands in hers. "He knows this. And I have to go now because I can't hold on any longer. I need to release my grip on this life. Just like you need to release your beloved Tony."

Alyssa shot a glance at Lauren, while emotion welled in her throat at the mention of Tony's name.

"Yes, I'm aware that you also haven't released someone because that love was the best you had. But Tony isn't here now. And he isn't the only one who can show you love. Let Ahmad in." She gestured toward her electronic tablet. "I've been reading your books to get a sense of who you are."

"That's fiction," Alyssa said as she sipped water from her bottle.

Lauren chuckled. "There's a little truth in every piece of fiction, yes?"

"Yes," Alyssa confessed with a smile of her own.

"Your books are very much a heartstrings thing," Lauren said, fingering the edge of the tablet. "I favor those old-fashioned Harlequins. The multicultural romances are a little different for me. But they are all love stories at the core."

"The people may look different, but the love is all the same," Alyssa agreed.

"But the writing is," Lauren replied, frowning. "Something changed between book three to book five."

Alyssa thought that over for a moment. "Before Tony came into my life, I was writing what I *wanted* to experience," she admitted. "After he … after he was killed, I was able to write what I had actually experienced."

"It shows. And now you'll have even more to write about. New adventures with a husband and a child. Now, if you don't mind, I'd like to have a word with Ahmad," she whispered. "Could you please take Taj somewhere for a while?

Alyssa stood from the bed so fast the nightstand shifted. "Wait." Alyssa shook her head. "I don't … what? And sure."

"Ahmad is a man who plays for keeps," Lauren warned. "When he wants a woman, nothing stands in the way of making her his. Nothing." Her eyes held Alyssa's for several moments. "He's loyal, has a bit of a temper, and doesn't like to share. So, this open marriage scenario never worked for him." Her smile widened. "Until now."

# Chapter 20

"They're not going to vacate the Power of Attorney. Your mother signed it. Two witnesses signed it, and Cain had Michelle Harris, someone you all went to school with at CVS, notarize her signature. It's fully legal. Unless you can get her to sign a new one, and have his signature on it as a witness, there's nothing you can do," Vikkas, the King of Wilmette, said into the phone from The Daley center in downtown Chicago.

"Why do we need his signature," Rahm questioned as he paced the hall of his home.

"It makes it airtight. He can't protest it later. But he could protest one we try to put in front of her right now. It'll simply be the battle of the POA's, and the lawyers will walk off with all of the money. We'll get a new one and have him involved," Vikkas answered. "Then, we'll have your mother on that plane and put Cain and all his madness behind you."

All while growing up, it was Cain versus Rahm. He never understood why. Maybe they got it honest. The brotherhood duel wasn't the only major thing that marked people who grew up in the Grand Crossing area. The name "Grand Crossing" came from an 1853 right-of-way feud between the Lake Shore and Michigan Southern Railway and the Illinois Central Railroad that led to a "frog war" and a crash that killed eighteen people.

The crash was the result of illegal construction of railroad tracks on behalf of the Illinois Central, across another railroad company's tracks which created hostilities between the two railroads. Lawsuits and appeals to civic transportation authorities escalated into the companies pitting their workers against one another with deadly results.

The area catered to the railroad workers of mostly Irish, Scottish, English, and German descent and were later joined by Swedes and Italians. African Americans began moving into the neighborhood from the overcrowded Black Belt and that's when Grand Crossing's White residents began to move out. Their "flight" allowed Rahm's grandmother to purchase her first property and raise her only daughter in a safe place that would afford her even better opportunities than her ancestors had.

Later, everyone pooled their resources to purchase a six flat, where the family resided on one side, Rahm on the top floor, grandmother on the first, and Lorraine in the middle; the other side was for families who brought in the funds to maintain the place. Unfortunately, Cain was promptly escorted off the premises after the fourth time one of his "cougars" vandalized the place to the tune of nearly twenty grand. That's when Aunt Alyssa moved into the building because tenants on the other side didn't feel it was safe. She was the only one of his father's side of the family that had anything to do with Rahm and Cain after their father was killed during the United States invasion of Panama.

Seems like Cain embraced the seedy side of the area's history since Grand Crossing also boasted one of the most notorious criminals—Al Capone, before he moved to Cicero. Rahm, his mother, and their grandmother, Mabel, had embraced the spirit of the hardworking railroad workers. Even now, with everything that had happened, Cain still hadn't caught on to the fact that living a criminal lifestyle wasn't the way to go. Yet, Rahm was the one who landed in prison. Life wasn't fair.

"I'm glad you're showing a lot more restraint with your brother than you had with Marilyn's ex-husband," Jai commented via the speaker phone.

"True that. He deserved that and then some," Rahm said. "Better be glad I was feeling generous. What he did to Marilyn was uncalled for …"

*Rahm had slammed Victor against the living room wall. The ex-husband had shown up at Marilyn's house without any warning, barged in, and went off about their youngest daughter. Wanda had gone to her father, spreading all manner of lies that escalated with her adding that Rahm had filled Marilyn's head with accusations that Victor may have molested her. If Rahm nearly choking him to death didn't get the message across to him that Marilyn was off-limits, the simple act of her straddling Rahm's lap and giving him the longest kiss possible, definitely put the nail right through his heart.*

This was a trip down memory lane he could not afford. He'd been away from Marilyn for two months. The thought of not being with her again caused more pain than he could handle at the moment. Getting his Mother here was his top priority. Dippin' wouldn't give a second thought about going after a woman in a fragile state.

*Chapter 21*

Alyssa and Charli stood by the granite bar discussing the night's event. Almost everyone had left Bliss 4 except them and, of course, Ahmad, who kept a watchful eye outside for both ladies and the few remaining guests.

"All right," Charli said, placing a hand on Alyssa's shoulder. "I'll say good night, and remember you have the upper hand."

Alyssa studied the smiling face of their sultry host while she waved to departing guests. Then she sighed and her brows furrowed. "I feel something for him, but I can't be sure it isn't because of all the wonderful things he's doing, or because the man is panty-dropping gorgeous, or because I'm in such a drought and he's the only sign of rain. He's already in a complex relationship with his ex, and he still loves her," she whispered. "I don't want to play games. This whole part of the relationship cycle is not in my wheelhouse."

"Have you ever heard of the Dance of The Seven Veils?" When Alyssa shook her head, Charli settled in to provide the explanation.

*The Dance of the Seven Veils was based on the biblical story of Herodias. She had an adulterous affair with her brother-in-law, Herod Antipas. Both divorced their spouses and married each other. John the Baptist scolded them because he felt the relationship was incestuous,*

*and in retaliation Herod imprisoned John. While this satisfied Herod, it
did not do the same for his wife.*

*At Herod's birthday party, his stepdaughter danced to entertain him
and his guests. Herod was so enchanted by the dance that he promised
her anything she desired. Her mother, Herodias, had the twisted and
wicked idea of suggesting that John be killed and his head severed as
a suitable prize for such a beautiful dance. John the Baptist's head was
cut off and delivered on a tray.*

"In this dance, as the veils are removed in a seductive manner, they
reveal this *korasion*—a prepubescent teenager or damsel—becoming a
woman. She was 'unlayering" her childhood and becoming naked to the
men.

"In the bible, seven means completion, and by the time she removes
the seventh veil she would be completely bare." Charli nodded, as she
focused on Alyssa. "Right now Ahmad is out there losing his mind
wondering if you are in here with someone else. For the two of you
this Bliss experience is like that dance. You've spent hours on the sofa
discussing all manner of things, oblivious to all the … interesting things
going on around you. You're unveiling each other one sheer piece of
material at a time, down to your truth, your spirit, and your nakedness.
Your pain."

Alyssa absorbed that for a moment, "When …" She inhaled, ignoring
Oliver's attempts to get her attention. "How could it have gotten so
deep, so fast?" She already knew his level of care for her safety and his
compassion played a considerable part. "So what you're saying is he's
more vested in alleviating my pain than he is with me."

"That's not what I'm saying at all." Charli placed a tray of food in
the fridge. "Opening to him, you being vulnerable touched him. Not
to mention his child loves you. Children and pets are a great judge of
character."

Alyssa removed a few grapes from the tray that was left on the
counter and popped one in her mouth.

"They say the way to a man's heart is through his stomach. I beg to differ. It's through his Mama or his child." She grinned. "Ask me how I know."

"That's not ... I wasn't—"

"That doesn't matter." Charli touched her shoulder. "That man is wealthy, talented, seasoned, and so handsome it hurts. You could do worse. You could have someone like Stewart or Oliver—all wealth and no common sense." She pushed Alyssa toward the door. "On that note, it's time to call this a night. Remember what I said."

"I'll try."

"Trying is lying," Charli snapped, her gaze narrowing to slits. "Whatever brought you all to this point, you'd better work it out."

Alyssa left the building and found Ahmad leaning against the car. He moved toward her, and from six feet away, he scanned her face and clothing so quickly that she almost missed it. His action hinted that he didn't want her to see that he was checking for signs that she'd enjoyed someone else's company.

"You know I'm perfectly fine staying at the hotel."

"I'm fully aware of that," Ahmad said, "but I promised Rahm that I would make sure you were well taken of. So, you will you stay at my house."

She found out after Rahm was on a flight to the States, and she couldn't protest, that he'd had a private conversation with Ahmad to move her from the hotel and into his home until he returned. She didn't know how she felt about the two of them conspiring in that manner, but she knew they both had her best interest in mind.

"Well I'm glad you put me up in your master bedroom, I suppose," she responded. "There's not enough white sage you can burn to get Susan's negative energy out of that place."

"I agree," he said chuckling. "That's why I'm camped out in the other guest bedroom. This house was built with escape in mind."

They drove in companionable silence for the entire ride, and their only connection was when he reached for her hand. She didn't resist his touch, and they stayed that way.

Ahmad ushered her inside the house, and they both went to their separate rooms.

Alyssa indulged in a hot bubble bath to ease her frustration. Then she applied lotion to her skin and curled up in bed thinking over tonight's events, waiting for sleep to find her. She had fallen for this man and didn't know how to reel her feelings back in. She had been open with him about so much. Those hours on the sofa were like ... therapy with a friend. There was so much about him to love.

A knock on the door brought an unexpected shiver of anticipation. "Come in."

Ahmad came past the threshold and raked her with his eyes. His intensity made her lower muscles clench.

"Undress for me," he said, his tone husky but commanding.

She froze. Every intimate interaction with him had taken place with a fabric barrier.

Fear gripped her in its ugly jaws. Only Tony had seen her bared to the world.

"I know the rules say I'm supposed to ask for permission, but this right here—in our space—is our thing. And I want to say it the way I would if we had no barriers between us. So please, Undress for me." He settled in the chaise situated near the middle of the floor, waiting. His gaze locked on her.

Alyssa slid out from under the comforter, threw her legs over the side, and stood. She hesitated as fear and confidence warred within.

Once, Tony had asked her to get in the shower with him. She tried, truly tried, but ended up standing outside the shower, mostly clothed, as she lathered him and explored his well-toned body. He had looked at her as though she had lost her mind. She regretted her actions to this day. Sometimes she wondered if he felt demeaned because she wouldn't do as he asked. His request was simple, but she couldn't bring herself to be that vulnerable to him. Now Ahmad was demanding more. Much more.

Neither Ahmad's posture nor focus wavered. Alyssa closed her eyes, reached for the hem of the flimsy gown, and inched it over her head. The bra and panties were still in place, and she hoped that he would at least allow them to remain.

Not so.

He settled in the chair as though he would remain there for the rest of the night until she did as he commanded.

She closed her eyes again, this time she reached behind her and unhooked the clasp. Her full breasts were free in a matter of seconds. She placed the bra next to the gown on the bed.

Desire flickered in his dark-brown eyes. And still, he waited.

Alyssa took a deep breath—actually several, and placed her hands on the thin waistband of her panties.

He watched the journey as she inched the material down her thighs, her legs, and lifted one foot, then the other to remove them from her body and also position them with their fabric cousins. Ahmad's gaze trailed a heated blaze from the top of her head down to the tips of her manicured toes.

She held her breath, willing the apprehension to drain away.

"Look at me," he said.

She did.

"Permission to touch you."

Alyssa wanted to say yes. Something wouldn't let the words come forth. Then that regret-filled memory flashed in her mind. If she had that day to do over, she would in a heartbeat.

The loudest sound in the room was the air. Her mind struggled to push the words past her lips. This was a new move of trust, that Ahmad wouldn't hurt her, that he wanted her, that she would allow the memory of Tony to fade and a new experience to replace the ones firmly etched in her soul.

Ahmad crossed the distance between them, his gait confident and purposeful, a far cry from what she felt. But she would try. She would love herself enough not to feel ashamed of any aspect of who she was. Even now, the full-length mirror presented a struggle every day. Her goal to stand, look at herself, and say that she loved herself, was still hard to reach. The issue at one point was having a man who loved her for her. *The real challenge is that I don't love me for me.*

"Permission granted."

He started by pulling her close to him, embracing her so tight she could feel the beat of his heart against her skin. His lips trailed a fiery path from the base of her neck to the small of her back, then down over her buttocks.

The scent of him was everything, warm and earthy. When he made the sensual trip in reverse, and they stood eye to eye, she buried her face in the wall of his chest, inhaling him.

"Did you ask permission to do that?"

Alyssa froze, looked up at him in time to see the corners of his lips lift in a smile.

Tension ebbed from her body as she sighed. "Permission to touch you?"

"Yes," he answered and drew her hand to the first button on his crisp white shirt.

She unbuttoned all of them, then they removed the garment together by sliding it down his muscled arms. While unveiling the masterpiece of his body a little at a time, he sometimes trembled under her fingertips, and she relished the effect she had on him.

Alyssa kept her gaze lasered on him as he removed the belt, unzipped his slacks, then shifted, so they slid to his feet. Gripping the waistband of his boxers, she slowly guided them over the tent created by his erection. She ran her fingertips across the veins and took in a sharp breath. His arousal made her head spin.

Breathing hard, Ahmad removed her hand from around him and kissed her fingertips.

She smiled then, realizing he was as affected by her as she was by him.

In the next instant, she was in his arms and he carried her to the bed, then gently positioned her so he could claim the space next to her. His heated gaze ignited her skin.

Ahmad traced a finger up her leg, then paused as he whispered, "Permission to kiss you?"

Her lips pressed to his, and he held on to her, first paying attention to the smooth skin of her shoulders before trailing down to her breasts, taking one brown bud into his warm mouth.

Alyssa squirmed, trying to contain the heat emitting from her center.

He spread her thighs, parting her folds and finding her delicate pearl, stroking her in a steady rhythm. He paused as her body arched toward him.

"My God," he whispered, as she trembled with his touch. "You're exquisite."

She recognized the sincerity in his gaze and allowed herself to relax and enjoy him for the first time.

* * *

Ahmad wanted to be inside her so bad it took every ounce of control he had to stay the course.

He pressed a finger into her moist heat and the walls clenched around it, drawing it in.

The whimper of pleasure called to him.

She gasped. "Do you have—"

"You gave me permission to touch you. This," he thrust the finger inside. "Is touch."

The orgasm that ripped through her also brought him extreme pleasure. Her body was so responsive to every nuance, every touch, every stroke. He enjoyed watching her open to him, wanted her as hot for him as he was for her.

Her nipples jutted toward him even as her eyelids fluttered and closed. Tomorrow, they would take it to another level. Taste. If she thought touch was amazing, she was going to lose her ever-loving mind.

Ahmad would make certain she belonged to him—*only* him.

# Chapter 22

Rahm had arrived at a location that he thought he wouldn't set eyes on for a long while. But here he was in Chicago at the Castle, staring at his brothers of the heart—Vikkas, Jai, Daron, and Shaz. The others— Reno, Grant, Kaleb, Dwayne, and Dro had pitched in their comments via a video conference. Each of them was formidable in black suits that were an outward show of unity when they came together to discuss an issue. They had laid out the beginnings of a plan, but none of it sat well with Rahm. Almost like rewarding Cain for his bad behavior.

"We have to play his game," Jai said to Rahm over the rim of a glass of Hershey's port. "I learned that from you and Marilyn."

*"Jai, you have to get your hands a little bit dirty if you're going to stay afloat,"* Marilyn suggested. *"They're stomping you into the ground because they know you're not going to do what it takes to beat them at their own game."*

And she was right.

"What your brother wants is money. Let's give it to him."

"No way in hell am I giving him anything more," Rahm protested, putting his back against the wall next to the screen. "He stole that settlement money. He took my mother from a safe place, put her in a dump, and leaves her alone for hours at a time. She could set the house on fire trying to cook because she'll forget she has something on the stove. No way do I want to reward him for what he's done."

"Are you finished?" Vikkas asked in a calm tone that nearly pissed Rahm off all over again. He, and his twin, Jai, were so much alike.

"Yes, I mean. Y'all know how I feel about this." He motioned around the table at the Kings. "So, we have to come up with another plan."

Jai pulled in a breath, expelled it, then spoke, "Like I said, what your brother wants is money. Let's give it to him,"

Rahm shouted, "I don't want you all to give him any money, either."

"Will you shut up a minute," Jai snapped.

Rahm flinched but clamped down on anything else he had to say.

"Daron," Jai said to the fedora-wearing man, who had a mysterious edge.

"What exactly do you have in mind?" Daron asked.

"Several things need to happen here," Jai answered with a glance at Shaz. "We need to have a new Power of Attorney signed, giving Rahm full responsibility for his mother's care. Also, we have to move her to Durabia. And, there's this Melvin Ogletree person we have to fix."

Frowning, Rahm asked, "Who?"

"You call him Dippin'."

"Oh, never knew his real name," Rahm said, still not understanding how they were going to pull this all together—so fast. Not to mention, he was still coming to terms with Marilyn ending their relationship. Now, his life was all about Durabia. He was all too happy to put America in his rear-view mirror, but not without her. She had given up a twenty-year career to be with him, along with doing what it took to help Jai snatch his medical center out of the clutches of a man hell-bent on forcing Jai to give up his position as a managing member of The Castle. There had to be a way to get her back.

How could life be going so well, then go so wrong? Now they wanted to give his brother money to make sure his mother was safe. In what world was that fair? His brother had done a lot of dirt in his lifetime, most of it he had gotten away with because he'd done the kind of things that didn't get a second or third look. He'd been with women—mostly older and established—and blew through their bodies and money as fast as he changed clothes. His good looks had opened doors faster than people realized they should have kept them closed, locked, and bolted.

"I know the problems," Rahm said. "Short of whisking her away on a private jet, I don't see how to get her out of here. Security said that some shady looking folks came looking for her only hours after Cain took her out of there. They wouldn't have made it past the front desk. But there's absolutely no security where Cain lives. It's only a matter of time before they find her. I'm not going back to Durabia as long as my mother isn't safe."

Rahm rubbed the back of his neck and watched Daron as he walked around the table.

"Here's what we're going to do," Daron said, sliding into the chair next to Rahm. "We'll put together five times what that settlement will bring and put that offer on the table. Then—"

"But—"

Vikkas held up a hand to halt any more words from Rahm. "But it will be on the condition that he executes a new Power of Attorney and a Family Memorandum of Understanding. One where you become responsible for your mother's finances and well-being, and two of us will be the designated caregivers if something happens to you."

"You all will do that for me?" Rahm looked at each of his brothers, and their collective nods let him know they understood. If tables were turned, they would all move heaven and earth for their own mothers.

"Vikkas and Jai have already agreed to it," Shaz said. "That's covered.

"You all worked out the plan before you came here?"

"Pretty much," Vikkas answered with a shrug. "That's just what we do."

Rahm walked around the table and gave each man a power fist. "Thank you, brothers. Much appreciated."

"Call Cain," Daron said, gesturing to his cell. "Have him to bring your mother here, along with her passport."

"Why?" Rahm asked as he returned to his seat at the table.

"You have to trust us, Rahm," Shaz said. "You know what we're capable of doing. Sometimes it's best that you don't know everything."

* * *

Cain skimmed the paperwork for the third time, then looked up at Shaz. "What's the catch?"

"Nothing. You get all of this," Vikkas replied from behind his desk, highlighting the cash portion. "When you sign this as a witness to the new power of attorney."

"A new one, huh?" His scrunched eyebrows and smirk revealed his skepticism over the process.

"Giving your brother the ability to care for your mother while over there," Shaz answered from the corner of the room where he stood.

"He can care for her," Cain said, grinning. "I just want the money."

Jai waved his hand over the stacks Vikkas had just pushed toward him. "And here it is. All yours."

"Isn't this kind of unethical?" Cain asked, eyeing the money like it was a long-lost lover. "As if you're buying my mother or something?"

"No, we're buying peace of mind." Vikkas smiled and handed Cain a pen to sign the power of attorney.

Cain steepled his fingers and glanced at Rahm who was still standing, "Why isn't he talking? Cat got your tongue, bro?"

"That's what he has us for," Vikkas answered.

"So, what, I sign this, and y'all just dance out of here with my Mama to Iran."

"*Our Mama*, and it's Durabia," Rahm corrected.

"Oh, so he can talk now," Cain taunted with a laugh.

"When it suits me," Rahm replied, leaning against the door jamb, ignoring the warning look Daron shot his way.

"A hundred grand." Cain stroked the bills on the top of the stack. "If you're willing to pay this much, then maybe y'all can come up off a little more dough."

Jai lowered his gaze and chuckled. "Where's Milan when you need her?"

All the Kings in the room laughed, causing Cain to frown and ask, "Who's Milan?"

Daron responded, "We were in a hostage situation earlier this year. Brought her brother and his thug buddies the exact amount they asked for to secure her release."

"Then he said the same thing you just said," Jai walked to where Shaz stood.

Cain glanced between the two men. "So why does she matter?"

Shaz pointed his trigger finger at him before saying, "She shot him."

Rahm's head whipped around. "Her own brother? Now there's a novel idea."

"You wish you had the balls," Cain said through his teeth.

"I have them, have yours too, since you were born without 'em, but I digress."

Jai put a hand on Rahm's shoulder but kept his focus on Cain. "Take the money, and let's be done with it."

Cain scanned the documents and their faces. "I'll sign it. But not here."

All of them fixed their gazes on him.

His lips lifted in a cat-that-ate-the-canary grin, and he threw his passport on top of the stack. "In Durabia. If it's good enough for my brother, it's good enough for me," he tossed out with a nod. "And I'll need just a little bit more travelling cash. About fifty large will do.

Vikkas, Jai, Shaz, and Rahm shared a speaking glance before Daron held up his hand to stop them from protesting as he said, with a wide smile, "No problem. Wheels up, but we have to make a little pit stop first."

Something about Daron's smile sent a shiver of alarm through Rahm.

# Chapter 23

"Today is all about taste," Charli said, gesturing to the table in the living room.

For the Paint and Sip portion of the Bliss event, an array of syrup, whipped cream, fruits, and chocolates were spread out in the center of the glass.

Alyssa was situated in her favorite spot on the sofa. She ignored the curious glares of those who waited for Ahmad to appear.

Couples filtered in gradually, and of course, her usual gawkers and Alyssa's "fan club" were in attendance. One brunette walked up and questioned why she had come alone, but before she could answer someone else wormed their way into the conversation.

"He finally let you out to play," Stewart said with a charming smile. "Loosened that control."

"He doesn't *let* me do anything," Alyssa snapped, smoothing the white semi-sheer maxi dress over her hips. "I choose what I do."

"Permission to taste?"

"No," Alyssa responded as she sat back and crossed one leg over the other.

Disgruntled, Stewart replied, "Then he has more control than you think," before he turned to leave.

"Like I said, I choose what I do," she said to his retreating frame. "You're upset that I won't choose you. It's not personal. Your whole air is entitled."

"And his is not?" he countered, turning to face her again. "Be honest. You're his, and you're just here to pretend you have some semblance of control. Pointing to the group of men he normally hung out with, I dare you to allow anyone here to explore some time with you. I double dare you."

He stormed past the men congregated near the threshold leading to the deck and whispered something along the way. Two of them gazed in her direction and walked purposefully toward the sofa, trying to block her regular holding ground.

Alyssa scanned the expectant faces in the room, then signaled to Charli to come forward. "Permission to hold you."

Charli quickly adjusted so that she was in Alyssa's arms, relaxed, and fully flushed.

"Am I cock-blocking?" she whispered against Alyssa's ear as a collective groan went up among the men.

"Indeed. Every single one of the men I don't want," Alyssa said, holding back a laugh. "Why do men assume that by giving an ultimatum, we would do exactly what they want?"

"Because the world revolves around men who can't fathom that they aren't the center of the universe," Charli replied. "Come, let's take this to a private room. Give them something to be really pissed about."

Charli led Alyssa upstairs, and Alyssa felt the glares of the men as they wound their way to the upper level to a series of private rooms. She chanced a glance in Stewart's direction, only to find his eyebrows raised and a smirk on his face, anger in those blue eyes.

They hadn't crossed the threshold to the room completely before she said, "What's holding you back, Alyssa?"

Alyssa averted her gaze to the massive beds, then sat on the chaise.

"There are any number of men—and women—who would love to play. But it is painfully obvious you are wired for monogamy, and so is he."

She inhaled and thought about Charli's question. "At first, it was because I was unsure of myself."

"And now?" Charli asked, listening to the voices at the bottom of the stairs.

"I don't like that they expect me to say yes, strictly because I'm the only one like me here. As though I should be grateful that they want me. It's a vibe and—"

"Like Stewart pointed out, Ahmad also exhibits that same sense of entitlement. Be honest. You want him, and you overlook that quality in him because he's familiar."

Alyssa licked her lips. "No, he feels like he's craving me."

"They're hungry, too," Charli said with a throaty chuckle. "You just don't want to feed them."

"I kind of thought there would be more ..." She pointed at herself.

"People of color?" Charli questioned.

"Yes. I don't want to feel like they were ..."

Charli moved closer to where Alyssa had settled. "Choosing you for that reason."

"Yes, like that. Look at you, finishing my sentences and all that. How did you know?"

She sat beside her on the chaise. "I've hosted hundreds of these. Trust me, you're not the only one who feels this way. The reaction may be a fetish or curiosity, but I'm thinking it's your vibe."

Their heads turned simultaneously as the voices sounded as if they were closer. Charli finished her thought. "Unapproachable, aloof, distant. Every man wants to be the one who draws you out. It's a challenge. And it's a damn good one. You have them so riled up that it's changed the entire dynamic of the event. Made it a hell of a lot more interesting."

"I don't know any woman who would intentionally be with a man because she's an experiment."

Charli gently patted Alyssa's hand. "Yes, they come with the expectation that every woman here is willing to accept them." Charli rose from the chaise. "You are very much proving them wrong—especially the mega-rich ones. Every single man here comes from money. And I'm not talking about lunch money either. This is supposedly a safe space for them as well. No is not a word they are used to. Right now they're down there massaging their egos. And it's a good thing."

"Famous last words," Alyssa replied with a smile.

Her phone vibrated. "Come, let's rejoin the group. We're about to have company. You've proven your point to them and him."

Charli and Alyssa tipped down the stairs to find Ahmad sitting on the sofa.

Conversations trickled to a halt as the two women stood at the bottom of the stairs.

"That's not what I was talking about," Stewart said dryly.

"I'm sure," Alyssa countered, giving him a megawatt smile. "Your answer will always be *no* simply because you expect me to say *yes*. Well, let me manage your expectation."

Gabe inserted himself in the conversation, saying, "The other men asked me to speak with you, to encourage you to be open to ... exploring."

Ahmad stood, but stayed near the sofa, his posture tight and coiled as though ready to spring if Stewart made one wrong move.

Charli elbowed her in the side, so Alyssa walked into Ahmad's arms. When she lifted her head from Ahmad's chest, Oliver gave her a withering glance.

"Everyone should be a little pissed right now," Stewart said, in a voice that carried over the music. "I'm just saying that if he doesn't have to play by the rules, why should we?"

Ahmad extracted himself from her embrace, looked at Alyssa, and said, "You're right. My apologies. It won't happen again." He locked gazes with Alyssa and asked, "Permission to taste you."

"Yes."

"Is that a hell yes?" he asked.

"Most definitely."

Ahmad guided her upstairs to one of the private bedrooms, closed and locked the door, eased her into a comfortable position on the bed, then slid off her stockings and curled them into his hands. He lifted her flowing white dress just enough to give himself a glimpse of heaven.

"You meant that kind of taste?" She gasped, trying to hide her discomfort and anticipation. "I don't think this is a good idea. I've got a lot going on down there. Fibroids, and—" She splayed her hands on his shoulders, intending to push him away.

"Honey, either you can let me check-up under the hood," he whispered in a husky tone. "Or I can just play with the toys on the dashboard."

Before she could make a protest either way, he shifted them both, and his lips were pressed up against her pearl, tongue flicking to the point she nearly jumped out of her skin.

"Ahmad," she purred.

He kept up the sensuous assault until the trembling started in her thighs and ignited the rest of her body. She had to grip Ahmad's shoulders to remain steady, or they would tumble to the floor.

"Ahmad," she screamed.

That vicious tongue traced the outline of her heated flesh.

Her moans rippled through the air, and soon all sense of time and space ceased to exist. Here, she was the only one who mattered, and he was the only one with intimate knowledge of this part of her. Something that, through their discussions on the sofa, he was well aware that her beloved Tony had never done. This way of pleasuring her was all his.

"Ahmad," she screamed.

He gave a low, throaty chuckle as he lifted his head and teased, "Say it louder for the people in the back row." He placed a gentle kiss to the inside of her thigh.

Ahmad went back to work. Soon, her thighs tightened around his head, her body writhing, trying to escape his ministrations.

"Please," Alyssa moaned.

"Please what?" he demanded.

She gasped for breath. "I can't take any more."

"Just a little more, baby, and I promise I'll stop. Let me pleasure you this way. I love the way you look when you're cumming. Say it."

"Yes," she said, oblivious to anyone or anything else. All she wanted was this moment with him.

The next orgasm stole up on her and spiraled outward from her core, making her scream. When she finally floated back into the room, Ahmad met her eyes, his gaze intense. "You are mine to please. Mine to hold. Mine to have. Mine to keep. All mine. Do you understand me?"

"Ahmad," she whimpered.

"Do you understand me?"

"Yes," came on a breathy whisper as she surrendered wholly to him. As she whimpered, he held on to her and closed his eyes.

"Alyssa?"

Her response was dreamy. "Hmm."

"Your pleasure is so important to me. I can't even put into words how I feel."

Alyssa's mouth opened, but she couldn't form the words for an adequate response. Especially since he had gone in for seconds ...

# Chapter 24

Daron and Rahm walked over to Cain, who stood next to Lorraine holding tight to the briefcase Vikkas had given him.

Daron beckoned to him and moved toward the door of Vikkas' office. "Ride with us, let's get the rest of your cash."

"Just us?" Cain questioned, his gaze narrowing on Daron.

"Of course, we're not going to do anything to you," Daron said with a smile that was unsettling. "I already let everyone know where we're going, and the Kings will watch your mother while we're gone," Daron responded.

"Fine, let's go." Cain glanced at his mother just before walking out the door. She was totally enthralled with whatever story Vikkas was telling.

They drove the one-hour distance from the airport to the three-level brick house in complete silence—each lost in their own thoughts. Rahm and Daron left the vehicle simultaneously, followed by Cain, who scanned the area, taking in the quiet tree-lined street. Daron waved at his silver-haired neighbor, then led the way to the side door. Rahm noticed that he had already disconnected the alarms discreetly from his tablet.

"Can we get this over with and back to the plane?" Rahm grumbled, staying in step with Cain to make sure his quick-fingered brother didn't pick up anything that didn't belong to him. He would not enjoy his fate if he stole from Daron.

"Man, this is a nice house," Cain said once they crossed the threshold and made their way into the state-of-the-art kitchen. "Mind if I look around a bit?" He took a gander at the windows and the door locks, causing Daron's lips to turn upward, almost as if he wanted that reaction.

"Actually, I do mind," Daron answered. "You're a guest. I would prefer if you stayed close."

He led them through a massive living and dining room area before entering his office.

Daron moved past the fully stocked bar to his desk and flipped a switch under the right-hand corner. If his set-up was anything like he had done for Rahm's quarters in The Castle, there would be two switches. One turned the cameras on and sent a silent alarm to the police department, the other turned the alarm on or off on the safe.

Then he removed the abstract painting from the wall.

"No one would ever know that was there." Cain's gaze bounced from the desk to the safe as though he was committing things to memory. "Ingenious." Then he whipped out his cell, turned his back to Rahm as he keyed in a few things to his phone.

Rahm wondered why Daron would be so careless as to allow them to see the combination and the set up. His brother was of particular concern and wouldn't hesitate to come back if he thought he'd get away with staging a break-in. How he managed to stay out of jail for so long was a miracle.

"That's the whole point, my brother," Daron said, "for no one to know." He turned his attention to Cain. "You asked for an additional fifty grand, right?"

Cain stepped closer, rubbing his hands together as if anticipating the feel of the money touching them.

"Daaaaayum, since you have that much," he said, staring at the rows of cash stacked in the safe, "let me get an additional five. After all, I'll be starting a new life as well. Need to live in big baller style like my brother." He glanced over his shoulder at Rahm before saying, "Then, once we land, you'll never have to hear from me again."

Glaring at Cain, he snapped. "Somehow, I doubt that will be the case."

Rahm glanced at Daron as he hesitated a few moments with his hand on one side of the safe, then closed it altogether and went to another safe on the floor and slid it to the side. Stacks and stacks of cash were piled up. Cain gasped and Rahm shut him down with a glare.

Daron grabbed a few and handed the money to Cain. "Our agreement was for five. That is what you're being given, along with the money Vikkas gave you earlier. That will suffice until you find adequate employment in Durabia." He gave Cain a cloth bag to hold the money and continued, "They don't allow freeloaders, so you must find work, even with this extra from my *special stash*. Now let's go. We have a plane to catch and documents to sign once we get on that plane."

"Why do you keep the money under the safe," Cain asked, trying to juggle the money and the bag.

"Thieves never think to look there, so that's where I keep the valuables," he said, clapping a hand on Cain's shoulder. "And it's why I don't even bother with real security. Let them have at what they can cart away. Saves time and keeps the police out of my business."

The three of them left the house and ten minutes into their drive to the airport, Cain said, "Stop here and let me out. I want to tell my boys 'bye before we leave. I'll be at the airport in a few."

Daron stopped the car next to the sidewalk. "Leave the bag. You have exactly one hour and no more to get back, or we will leave you. Understood?"

"Yeah, man, don't sweat it. I'll be there." Cain jumped out and walked across the street to a group of men idling on the corner, all while Rahm was trying to reach Marilyn.

"Somehow, I don't get a good feeling about this," Rahm said as they drove off. He continued to watch his brother in the rear-view mirror. Cain and four of them hopped into a car and took off in the opposite direction.

Daron responded with a chuckle. "Don't worry, everything will be fine. I'm sure he won't let this perfect opportunity pass him by."

Rahm studied Daron for a few second. "I feel that has a double meaning, and knowing you, I'm sure it does."

* * *

"Daron, I know we have a deadline," Rahm said looking straight ahead at the road.

"But you want to go see Marilyn, right?" Daron finished his sentence for him. "Another sprung one."

"You can't talk," Rahm shot back. "Cameron has you the same way."

"Facts," Daron said, laughing.

"I have to try one more time, since we're here." He turned to face Daron in enough time to see his grin. "I've been trying to reach her for hours, and she hasn't answered. Time for me to slide through and make a play."

"My man," Daron said, extending one hand for a fist bump.

Daron drove across town to Marilyn's place and barely parked the car before Rahm jumped out. "At least give me time to stop the car," he joked.

Rahm ran up the stairs and knocked on the door. Just as he lifted his hand to knock again, it opened.

"I thought you were in Durabia," Marilyn said while she waved at Daron. "Come in," she said, before turning to walk inside.

The amazing sexy woman he loved was in full effect, but looked as though she'd been crying. Her creamy skin had a flush of color; some of the curves that he loved being wrapped around were a little less prominent. She'd lost weight and knowing it might be because of their relationship, was painful to consider. Or was there something else she hadn't told him?

Rahm followed behind her but didn't wait for the door to close before he pulled her into his arms. "Marilyn please consider coming with me. You can pack a bag, and we can buy whatever else you need there. I want you with me," he said, as he closed the door.

"Don't give up on us, baby," he whispered against her skin. "At least come and see things first, then make a decision."

She walked back to the door and opened it, "You still don't get it. Everything is not about you and what you want." She ushered him outside. "See you around, Rahm," and with that she closed the door.

Rahm called her name several times to no avail, then returned to the car with a heavy heart. "That didn't go so well," he said to no one particular, "Let's go."

"It will work out, bro," Daron replied, placing a hand on his shoulder.

They rode to the airport in silence.

* * *

Cain made it back to the plane with only three minutes to spare. For some reason, he had a larger bag than when they left him over forty-five minutes ago.

"What's with the extra luggage?" Rahm asked, his glare never leaving his brother's.

"Just more clothes, that's all," he responded, holding it tighter. "I don't want to spend all the money on buying new clothes. I have to make that last … until I find a job, Or maybe you can break me off with some more cash."

Daron walked between them, holding his hands out. "You two can argue more once we are in the air, but for now, just let it be." He put his gaze on Cain, "Milan isn't the only one who knows how to shoot family. Cain killed Abel, but I'm thinking that if you cross us, it'll be Cain that will see the business end of a Smith & Wesson. And remember, you're not my brother."

# Chapter 25

Daron made a call right before take-off, then settled in for the thirteen-hour ride by placing his fedora over his face and sliding straight into sleep.

Vikkas and Jai fell into a discussion regarding helping a doctor get out of a contract with a woman named Susan.

In their talking back and forth, Rahm overheard them say that the woman had fled Mississippi for Durabia and attached herself to an affluent doctor there. She had done horrible things to a wealthy patient, including having his daughter locked away, and he was still trying to get to her.

Rahm took the seat next to his mother and made sure they were nowhere near Cain, who was overjoyed with the wide selection of movies. A tense vibe hung in the air that Rahm felt down to his bone marrow.

Paying his brother for his mother's freedom sounded more like slavery than anything. Things like this were never supposed to happen. Prison had taught him a lot. Like how to take a dim view of his brother's schemes which started when he landed his first cougar in high school. Rahm understood that prison was the biggest con game going. On the day he was released, he explained a lot of it to his Aunt Alyssa when she picked him up.

*"They put prisons in rural places where White Republicans created whole communities. They build a core based on the prison system—basically slave labor. The town might hold two, maybe three thousand people, but the prison being situated there means that number jumps up to six thousand people. That means the town receives and reaps the financial benefits of those six thousand, instead of the true count from people who actually reside there.*

*"The experience was horrible for those who came from low-income families. They landed inside, and people couldn't put money on their books. They lose touch with family and friends. Part of the reason they're there in the first place is lack of money and opportunities, which led to bad decision-making."*

His mother did everything in her power to ensure that Cain and Rahm wouldn't fall prey to the things that would land them behind bars. Drugs. Gangs. Murders. None of that was in their vocabulary. So how was it that he, not his always-on-the-brink-of-trouble brother, ended up on the wrong side of the bars?

Seems like life wanted him to make up for lost time. Now, after the Kings of the Castle made inroads to build a legacy relationship between their interests in America and Durabia, the outlook for Rahm was brighter than ever. The one day that stood out for him most was when an all call came from Dro and everyone answered and were on private planes to Durabia in no time flat.

At the wedding of Kamran Ali Khan and Ellena Kiley, Rahm was able to see how royalty lived. The entrance of the palace was spectacular. But the room for the ceremony had been transformed into a wonderland of lilac, purple, creams, and gold, plus flowers galore. Even that didn't compare to the Kings, Queens, Knights, and Ladies who rolled up in the palace as if they owned it, taking their rightful place beside Ellena. The solidarity was to let the ruling Sheikh know that she had family and protectors.

Everyone thought her to be a commoner until Khalil Germaine handed over her dowry of eighteen-million dollars. These were some badass men to roll up in a palace, commandeer the wedding, and turn it into a Chicago Style party. After the wedding, things grew a little shaky because Kamran's sisters-in-law became jealous and feared their husbands might lose the throne. They took matters into their own hands allowing his brothers to show their true ruthless nature. After being wrongly denied, Kamran ascended to the throne and the shift in the kingdom was still being felt. With Ellena's influence, Sheikh Kamran had established several crisis centers for women and was changing some of their customs regarding women's rights and those for ex-patriates.

Now Rahm had to wonder what they were doing when it came to elder care or people with health issues like his mother. He didn't even bother to look into it, because she would live with him and he'd bring in round the clock companions to help with her care.

Cain's delight with something he saw on the screen had him cackling, which brought Rahm back to the happenings on the aircraft. The private jet that belonged to Khalil Germaine, the founder of The Castle, had the kind of luxury only the mega-rich could buy.

Rahm sighed, wishing Marilyn was on her way to Durabia with him. The thought of navigating the dating scene again was not appealing in any way. He'd been with East Indian, Latina, straight off the boat Russians, Lithuanian, Bosnian, Polish, and found that White women had an entirely different attitude. They hadn't been through the same struggles as Black women. Most times, their families had things set. Families that were like, '*here's a house, here's one hundred grand to start your life and come out of college with your education paid for in full.*' Life was easier for them because financially, their parents had been set in life, and they made sure their children had a hand up as well. At least from what he'd found in his relationships, they were a lot better off than a young woman from a Black family. So their ease into life is a lot different, and so is their entrance into relationships.

Rahm had watched as his mother struggled paycheck to paycheck. Then his brother preyed on women. He wanted none of that for himself or his children and thought he had everything all set with Marilyn, for them to live and thrive in a place where he wouldn't be tainted by his past. A place where everything was open to them and for them.

Now she wanted to back out of the deal, and his heart was suffering the first heartbreak since his brother's betrayal sent him to prison. He was happy to have his mom back, but how would he get the woman he loved to join him? Better yet, where was his brother going to live when they arrived in Durabia?

Certainly not with him.

# Chapter 26

Ahmad and Alyssa didn't make it to the stairs before Charli went off the deep end.

"You five are not allowed to attend the Bliss 6 and 7 events," she roared.

Several of the men edged away from her.

"Your actions here tonight and last night were selfish and is not what these events are about. I have to protect the women here from such blatant disregard for their feelings. I am asking you to leave. You are not learning anything from this experience because you don't believe the rules apply to you. That's part of what's wrong with the world today."

"We paid," Oliver protested.

"I will refund every single dime," Charli barked.

"Can I at least—"

"No. Gather your things and be gone," she said, whipping out her cell. "Please do not make me have to involve the authorities."

The men grumbled, as they reluctantly complied.

"To anyone else who fails to keep to the letter of what these events are about, please feel free to join them."

No one else moved.

"This is the problem now." She moved toward the center of the living room. "Men who can't handle rejection. Men who are giving lip service to this process, but in their hearts aim for something else. Your power is not absolute. Your privilege is not absolute."

"Give women the chance to know if being with you is right *for them.* This is why men are constantly in trouble when it comes to consent. You can't take a no gracefully, feeling she must say yes, simply because you asked, and you have a dick." Charli grabbed her crotch to emphasize her point. "Hearing 'no' is a good thing. You need to earn that yes, not expect it."

Alyssa agreed with her sentiments. One of the reasons she had shied away from dating was because of the news reports of men losing their minds when women rejected them. One man shot a woman in a bar because she told him she already had a mate. Another shot a woman and her child because she said she did not want to take his number.

But the greater majority that inspired fear were those men who tried to kill—and those who did kill—women who were fed up enough to leave a bad relationship. Why men would be so fixated on one woman when women outnumbered them nearly seven to one in America, was beyond reason. When it came to men, they had plenty of fish in the sea. Women had slimmer pickings, and that was the reason some stayed in relationships far past their expiration date.

"Fragile little egos," Charli taunted. "You're not after the women who actually want you." She shook her head. "No, you spent your time lamenting and being angry at the only one who didn't. How sad." She gestured to the door and the burly men who walked into the room. "Make sure they're off the premises."

"You're welcome to stay in one of the private rooms," Charli said to Ahmad, when he descended the stairs with Alyssa.

"We can't stay all night," Alyssa answered. "Taj is expecting us for breakfast in the morning."

Just when he believed his heart couldn't open any wider, this. She was putting her own pleasure aside because she remembered his son. Gently, he squeezed her hand. "I promise you we will leave at first light."

"All right," Alyssa agreed with a dreamy smile.

Ahmad watched as everyone went back to what they were doing, but a few whispered in one corner, shooting darts at Alyssa with their eyes.

He beckoned for her. "Come."

She glanced down at his hand, then at his face. "Hell, if I could come that way …"

Ahmad threw his head back and laughed.

# Chapter 27

Clearing customs was a faster process than expected. Almost unnaturally so. Once Cain and his mother signed the Power of Attorney, only then did they move into the area where a limousine awaited them. Rahm trailed Daron and Shaz, who seemed to be walking with a slower gait than usual.

He kept pace with them, but also focused on the officers who appeared from the opposite direction with a more purposeful walk, almost as if they were on a mission.

"Cain Fosten," the tallest of the officers said.

"That's me," Cain said.

"You're under arrest for smuggling counterfeit currency."

"What … wait."

The first two had him in cuffs in the time it took to blink. The other searched the bag and pulled out the stack of additional cash that he brought with him, against Daron's advice. Cain said he was going to hang out in Durabia for a while and see if it would suit him permanently. Not a prospect that Rahm welcomed.

"Counterfeit?" Cain shrieked. "What the hell are they talking about?"

Daron glanced at Rahm and winked. Realization slammed into Rahm, and it took everything in him not to smile.

*I suggest you leave this in your apartment until you get back.*

*Are you sure you want to bring all that cash on the plane?*

Daron and Shaz had both offered a slight warning that Cain had chosen to ignore.

"What is the penalty for this kind of offense?" Rahm asked, watching his brother struggle against the two officers.

"About six years," Jai replied. "Give or take." He threw in between tapping his phone screen.

*Oh, that's cold.*

"I got the money from them," Cain yelled, struggling against his constraints.

"Are you accusing members of the royal family of having counterfeit money?" one of the officers said. "They have millions of dollars."

"What would they need with fake currency," the other scoffed.

"Royal family?" Cain replied, giving Rahm and the others a disdainful glance.

"Keep it up," Vikkas said. "Slander will add another ten years to your sentence."

Cain's angry glare locked on Rahm. "You knew. You knew they would do this to me."

"No, not at all," Rahm said, leaning in to whisper. "Karma comes with a calling card that says, 'remember that shit you did.'"

They carted Cain off with him screaming all the while that he wouldn't survive in a place like a prison. Men who looked like him were vulnerable—pretty boys. He didn't know what prison was like in Durabia. Still, the one misconception that was quickly negated when Rahm landed in Menard was that homosexuality was prevalent.

Gay people had to shower by themselves or with other gay people. They couldn't just hop in the shower with a straight person. That lifestyle was frowned on by everyone—Christians, Muslims who made up a large part of the population, and gang organizations. The gay prisoners didn't get beaten up, but were ostracized by the general population.

From what Rahm understood about Durabia, which followed the prevailing laws of Islam, the case would probably be the same.

"What's going to happen to him," Rahm asked, putting a vise grip on Vikkas's arm.

Rahm glanced at Shaz and Vikkas, but Daron was the one who answered, "They are going to give him a plea deal where he will stay, doing nearly a year or two of community service, finish his education, things like that. More years for him to get his act together. Whatever you recommend is what we will do. So, what will it be?" Daron asked with a knowing stare.

"Wait." Rahm laughed. "You mean, I'm in control of his life?"

"Privileges of being a Knight in the royal family," Vikkas replied with an ear-to-ear grin.

*Chapter 28*

"I asked you to leave."

"I just asked a question," Oliver protested.

Charli glared at him as if he'd grown two heads, "What is the response when anyone here says no?"

He lowered his gaze. "Thank you for taking care of yourself."

"Twice you've tried to persuade her into a 'yes' after she clearly declined your offer. Thank you for coming."

"But—" Stewart began.

"You know the rules. Goodnight, and thank you for coming."

"What about the rest of the events?" Oliver whined. "I paid good money to be here." He looked around for others to join him, but they shied away, knowing Charli had already kicked several out before them.

"You are not allowed to return to any Bliss workshop, here or in America."

"This is unfair," Oliver yelled. "Why come to an event if you're not—"

"Engagement is not necessary," Charli shot back, beckoning for the security guards. "Have you ever considered that being here was her way of overcoming a challenge, and she simply needed time to adjust? That's what this exercise is all about. Learning what boundaries are. You are not ready. If anyone here thinks this is purely a free-for-all for you to get your freak on, then the door is that way." She thumbed in that direction. "This is a lesson in consent and boundaries. Someone's presence here does not constitute consent, is that clear? We made that abundantly clear in the Opening Circle, but I guess it bears saying again. Consent is *required*. Boundaries are to be *respected*. Is that clear?"

"Ooooh wee," Sherry, a platinum blonde whispered. "Never seen Queen C so upset."

"She has every reason to be," Alyssa said. "They're assholes. She knows it. They know it."

"They're rich enough to have any woman they want," Sherry said. "They're fixated on you because you're not allowing anyone a chance to get close. You're a challenge. They want us because easy is their way of life. They can buy anything."

Alyssa faced the rest of the guests. "Let me tell you all something. I came here, and to the other ones, because this is a *safe place*. It took a lot of courage for me to come to a group of total strangers and learn to open up again. To get over my fears of being intimate. It doesn't require that I prove anything to anyone here. I have to prove something to myself." She left Ahmad's side. "Did you even listen to the women here in the Opening Circle? Ninety-five percent of them felt safe enough to mention that they'd been raped. Did you catch that? No! You were too busy mapping out your plans for your own gratification."

Most of the guests stood with their mouths open, while a few of the privileged mumbled something she couldn't catch as they anticipated the end of her speech.

Alyssa placed her hand on her chest as she continued. "See, I didn't share my story. I was thirteen, and I went to the house of this boy, John, who I thought loved me. What would I know about love, right?" She frowned, remembering how naïve she had been. "Well, I gave him my virginity, but that wasn't enough. He had three friends—two older boys and one of their little brothers show up when he was done. They wouldn't let me leave until they were finished. Then they beat me to make sure I kept my mouth shut." She pulled up her sleeve to show the scar that remained on her arm, "I had a hard time explaining where those bruises and that black eye came from. I was scared to go to school because I thought it would happen again. For three years, I lived in fear, and I would run home every day, so none of them would catch me and do it again."

The room was so quiet, she only heard the hum of the refrigerator.

"I swore then I would never let another man take what I wasn't willing to give." She gestured to Charli. "This place, this experience, was supposed to help me with becoming whole again. I lost the one man who had made me feel beautiful and I didn't think it was possible to feel anything close to that." She locked gazes with Ahmad. "I was wrong."

A few whispers echoed, but it didn't matter. By forcing her to constantly assert herself, those men had ruined this beautiful experience for her—and others.

"You want to know why I didn't choose you? I don't feel safe with you." She pointed at Oliver, Gabe, and Stewart. "Despite knowing the rules, you and your vibration don't feel safe for me. Safety has been so much a priority that I haven't let anyone get close to me in years." Purposely, she moved to the man she desired. "You think I chose Ahmad because he's handsome, wealthy, or because he's a person of color. No, it's because he makes me feel safe, and cared for, and cared about. And that was hours before we made it to this place."

She stood straight, with a fierceness she didn't feel and studied every face in the room. "I was here, looking for myself—some part of me that I lost—I didn't realize that doing the healing work restored the first part, but Ahmad is giving me the rest." She pointed her finger at all of the men. "If you've ever, ever overruled a woman's no—and deep down you know that you have, realize you did the same thing to her, that those boys did to me. It didn't matter that I had consented to one of them, that didn't mean all of them could have a turn."

She grimaced at the pain the memories brought forth. "And who could I tell? I wasn't supposed to be there. I was supposed to go to the grocery store and come right back. I disobeyed my mother, so I deserved it, right? All these years, I thought that what they did to me was my fault for that reason alone."

"Honey." Ahmad pulled her trembling body against him. "I'm here. I'm here."

The hurt continued to pour from her lips as she locked a tear-filled gaze with the men who were the worst of the culprits. "You're supposed to be our protectors and defenders. Our brothers, fathers, cousins. But who protects us from you? We can't even be safe in places that tell you how much we need to understand consent." Tears streamed down her cheek. "I was so ashamed when Charli asked if we could hold a Bliss event, one geared to the Black Community. I broached the subject with a few of the guys that I play Bid Whist with. The idea of consent was so blurry, their intent so ugly, I knew I couldn't subject my sisters to that. They said, and I quote, 'Oh, I'm gonna get me some. Those men—men, I've known for years, and their response was to assert that they were going to get some ass before it was over. No different than those four boys." Her flawless pink nail pointed at each man who had come for her. "No different than you all here today. So I'm finding that this disregard isn't a Black or white thing. Rich or poor, even. It's all about that little piece of meat between your legs, and the brain attached to it believing life and death is in the power of its existence."

The ticking of the clock grew louder in the silence. "So don't get upset that I chose Ahmad. Try to figure out *why* I chose him." She traced Ahmad's muscular chest with one finger. "He is awesome. He is compassionate. He is intelligent. He is loyal. He is fine as hell, and most of all, he respects my boundaries and asks what I want to do." Her death stare made Oliver squirm. "You want it that bad, huh? You've been sex starved all your life—and must have me, right?" She waved her arm and stopped where each woman was situated. "When all these other women consented."

"But they're not you," Stewart said, bypassing the bodyguard to move further into the room.

*This asshole didn't hear a word I said.* Alyssa shook her head and sank on the sofa. "You know what? Since you want to make this all about wet ass and slick dick. I'll save you from yourself. Be quick about it." She raised her white dress halfway up her thighs and smiled in an inviting way.

Chest heaving, Oliver glared at Ahmad for the longest time, then smirked and moved forward. But it was Stewart who brushed past him on his way to the sofa.

"I swear on everything I consider holy," Ahmad said through his teeth, but loud enough for it to echo through all the rooms. "You lay one finger on her, and I'll toss your ass over that fucking balcony."

Everyone froze. Oliver threw a panicked gaze at Ahmad and stepped back, quickly shoving his hand in his right pocket.

"And just know that when you were done," she said with a glare at Stewart. "I was going to need Ahmad—a *real* man—with some *real dick*, because I'm pretty sure you were about to give me some pussy."

Pin drop quiet was an accurate assessment of the lack of noise around them.

"And I'm pretty sure you're thinking that she has one of those already," Ahmad said to Stewart and Oliver, trying to keep his smile from taking over his face. "But I named hers … Heaven. And I promise you that it—and she—are divine."

"Damn that was cold," Charli said, grimacing along with a few other women before she said, "Every night you come in here packing wood, swearing you can hammer nails with it." She made of show of peering down at Stewart's crotch as she planted herself between the two men. "Right now, you're hanging so low you could stir coffee at the equator.

"That's if he had enough of one to begin with," Shelly chimed in, putting a stony glare on Stewart, who had turned several colors before landing on beet red.

The room erupted in momentary laughter as Ahmad approached Alyssa.

"Enough! This is no laughing matter," Stewart roared, and everyone froze again.

Ahmad's gaze connected with Alyssa's. "Don't you *ever* do that again," he warned her, moving forward to take his rightful place beside her. "I know you didn't mean it. You didn't want it. You were testing their sense of decency. Baby, They. Have. None!"

Ahmad let those words ride around the room, before adding, "They're not going to get this in one night, from one woman. Every woman in this camp needs to be singing that same song—I am worthy, and I deserve a man who knows what that means."

He smoothed her dress down over her thighs. "See, they're the type of men who look the other way when their homeboys slide up in their sisters—even when she says no. And, they're the type of men who'll ask, 'well, what were you wearing?' What were you doing in his room? Damn the fact that she said 'no'."

Ahmad's knuckles turned white from the force in his fist, probably with the need to punch one of them. "So, no, honey. I know how you meant it, but he was going to take you up on that offer. And I was going to need bail money." He pulled up her sleeve again to display the scar. While everyone else gasped, Ahmad leaned over and placed several kisses on that very spot. "This doesn't diminish your beauty. It shows me survival, persistence, and tenacity. It tells me you are loved by the Most High. Even though your heart is bruised and scarred, you're still here and that, my love, is beautiful."

Some of the women let loose with a few "awwws" and "oooohs."

"He's right," Alyssa explained, glancing at the faces around them. "I understand that women and men are wired differently, but please consider that we—and I mean women—come here because it is the one place that we shouldn't experience the things we have in the past. The *one* place we're not simply a piece of meat or something for you to stick your dick into. We'd like to be more than just that." She glanced to where Oliver, Stewart, and Gabe stood. "We deserve more than that." She turned to Ahmad, whose eyes were glassy with unshed tears.

He said, "May I have permission to …"

She was in his arms in the time it took to breathe.

"Permission to embrace you," Charli said.

"Yes."

Charli wrapped her arms so that Ahmad was sandwiched between them. Then another woman asked the same question. And yet another. Until every woman in the room surrounded Alyssa, holding her. They stayed that way for a while as she cried for that little girl who had been devalued in that way. Three years of believing they would snatch her on the way home. Three years of leaving school early so she would have a head start to safety.

"Thank you. Thank you so much," Alyssa said in a shaky voice when they finally pulled apart. "I didn't mean to—"

"It's all right." Charli placed a hand on Ahmad's shoulder. "You take her home."

"Yes," he said, but held on to her a while longer. "I'm sorry no one was there to protect you. I'm here now. And I will do my best to make sure you're always protected and safe—even from me."

Alyssa buried her head in his chest and stayed there for as long as she could.

# Chapter 29

"You managed to get yourself kicked out of a Paint & Sip party? Seriously, Oliver?" Susan snorted before emptying her wine flute and waving it at the bartender. She turned to face the young stallion with his shoulders hunched at the bar.

Any other time she would have jumped at the chance to raise a young one to her hand—making him be what she wanted him to be. A toy, nothing more. *Just look handsome and take care of my needs. You can do that, right?*

Susan squirmed a little on the ebony barstool relishing the idea of riding his perfect Grecian nose as he drowned in her juices. Uncrossing her legs with agonizing slowness, Susan ran her black stiletto up the back of his thigh and he winced.

"All you needed to do was get close to her and during that …" She lifted a questioning eyebrow.

"Sensual Body Painting," he mumbled as he downed another shot and made circles on the cocktail napkin with the glass.

"Slide that syringe into her and she would no longer be a problem," Susan said. "They would blame any one of the people there. Explain to me what happened."

"You get a pallet and a body. You can do cosplay or just you know…

paint and stick the tip … with permission of course, but she wasn't into it. All her attention was on the Big Shot Sand Dweller, Ahmad. He would not leave her side. And when he wasn't there, Charli took up residence in that space next to her. I asked her nicely several times. Every single time it was no. I barely get the words out and she's cock blocking. Denying me. Me, of all people. I *never* get turned down."

Susan chased the bitter bubble of hatred rising in the back of her throat with a sip of white zinfandel the bartender supplied after removing her empty flute. Oliver was a wealth of information this evening but not a single ounce of action. Priming the pump was only half the battle. The first night she met with him in the cocktail bar of the hotel she was staying in was like providence. Jameel had come through for her. With a few more drinks, the man's envy rushed forth with just enough force to blunt hers.

Alyssa was nothing to look at, but she managed to bewitch Ahmad. It wasn't right and certainly not fair. After everything she had done to set him up, that wench came along and scooped him up! Susan was a king maker for Christ's sake. Susan saw the greatness in men and made them better. Was it too much to ask for them to show a little gratitude? First Chaz, now Ahmad, and now this. It couldn't do. No, this was unacceptable. Susan had made plans and that … that woman just …

Life seemed to be on repeat. She'd had a similar experience with Amanda McCoy who snatched Chaz right out from under Susan's nose. The things that Susan had done to "Mandy" were in and of themselves deplorable, but necessary. Still didn't work in the end though. She had everything well in hand and on the right track with Ahmad. Then Lauren and Taj showed up. Then Alyssa slid into the picture. What kind of luck was Susan having right about now? She certainly shouldn't make any trips to Vegas anytime soon.

Susan tilted her head and continued to stroke the back of Oliver's calf with the tip of her shoe, barely listening to his diatribe.

"You know, something should be done about rule breakers like her. Her kind, they never seem to get it; their purpose, I mean. Once they outlive it … they get comfortable like good old sheep, but even dogs know when to heel. Her kind doesn't. All they have to do is crawl back to their ghettos and stay there, die there with their pimp boyfriends and a hundred babies. I pay enough into the system for them. Sure, they can be educated, and some are even beautiful and a real credit. But we all know where they really belong."

She nodded as her smile slid behind the wine flute once more.

Oliver looked up from his drink and swayed a little before focusing on her. He was so deep into complaining; he didn't have eyes for anyone else in the bar. "Too right. I mean who does she think she is, telling me no? I have money. I can buy and sell her twice. All I asked was that she play by the rules. She even offered herself to me, but he stepped in. Threatened me in front of all my friends."

He blew out a long slow breath then continued with, "She made a joke of me in front of my friends. Then he took her upstairs. We could hear her screaming his name. That bastard! We tried to go up there. Next thing you know, Charli is tossing me out on my ass while Mr. Big Shot is in between Alyssa's thighs, and it was my turn," he yelled making some of the other patrons turn in his direction. "My turn."

Susan patted his shoulder and gave a pitying smile to the onlookers.

"Something should be done about people who don't remember their place, don't you think?"

Oliver pointed at the shot glass, and the bartender took his time heading their way. The young, ginger-haired man slung a dishtowel over his shoulder.

"Sir, I think—"

Oliver swung his head in the bartender's direction. "You don't get paid to think. I own this hotel. I pay your salary, so I own you, too," he growled. "Fill the fucking glass and leave the bottle."

The bartender chuckled as he bit his lip and filled the glass, then set the bottle aside. He pulled the towel from his shoulder and handed it the female bartender before removing his apron. "He may own this dump, but he doesn't own me. Put my paycheck in the mail, Tina. I'm out of here."

Susan took a swig of her wine, shrugging at the wicked shudder of bliss that crawled up her spine. Her father taught her all about fishing when she was a girl.

*Some fish don't like certain worms, honey. Put the right kind of nightcrawler on the hook and hell itself won't break the grip.*

"Women like Alyssa are such teases. I mean look at the news. They're always pregnant, so you know that has to be proof they're all hot in the tail," he continued, as she feigned interest in the conversation until he said, "I should just take what I want. It was ours, by right, years ago. Maybe, I'll go back there and take it and then finish her off."

Susan glanced around the room to see if anyone heard him, then leaned in closer. "Make her pay for forgetting her place, huh?"

Oliver wrapped his lips around the shot glass and tossed his head back, emptying the contents.

Susan clapped as he set the glass on the counter and bowed. "Make them all pay for having no manners and forgetting their betters."

Susan finished her wine and slid from her chair, brushing up against his body. Oliver grabbed a handful of her bottom, and she squealed, throwing her arms around his neck.

"Every night it's the same, Susan. Ever since that man put you up here in my hotel. He called in a favor to get you here. First, you asked me to take care of one issue, then before I could clear things up, you throw in another. You really want him that bad?"

Oliver rose and staggered toward a table, but Susan stiffened in his grip and shoved at his chest. "If you're going to make fun of me."

He sobered up as he brought her closer. "No honey, not at all. I'm with you and all … I just need assurances."

"Like?" She waved one hand to encourage him to speak as she moved him toward the back of the room and got them situated at a small table.

Oliver swallowed hard and licked his lips before leaning forward to whisper in her ear. "If I give you what you want, will I get what I want?" He leaned back and searched her eyes. "The boy and his mother aren't a problem. Call it pest control, but how can you be sure he will leave Alyssa and come to you?" he asked with a sly grin.

Susan pushed him further into the booth and fixed her clothes. She smoothed her hair and waved at the female bartender. The woman pointed to the empty wine flute on the bar, and Susan nodded.

At last she turned to look at Oliver, who ogled her like a smitten puppy. Cringing inwardly, she ran her thumb over the tip of his damp, hot knob. "You'd be amazed at what a little euthanasia can get you these days. Grief is a tool. Make yourself indispensable and even the hardest nut cracks." She pinched him for emphasis, making him jump before rubbing an apology into his skin. "Do it well enough. I get my prize and you get yours."

Oliver put his head on her shoulder and ran the back of his hand over the sensitive, exposed flesh at the top of her collar.

Susan swallowed hard to suppress the gorge rising to the back of her throat.

"Where's my retainer?" Oliver asked, hooking his finger in her shirt and peering down the front of it.

Susan scanned the crowd and cleared her throat before giving him a tight smile. "I'll let you pick a hole, if you make it look like an accident."

Oliver fell back in the seat and ran a pasty, white tongue over his lips. "Pictures too."

The sing-song quality in his voice made her stomach turn. She forced another smile to her lips. "Do it well, Oliver, and we can make a porno."

# *Chapter 30*

"That had to be the fastest court hearing on the planet," Rahm said.

"Things work a little differently here," Vikkas explained.

"Sounds like this was a set-up from the start." He stared at Vikkas and Jai.

"We improvised," Vikkas replied as they made their way down a flight of stairs and out the front door of the Justice Department. "The actual plan was for him to get his justice served on American soil. Prisons here are like luxury hotels."

Rahm paused and waited for the two officers behind them to pass. "Well, what now? 'Cause he can't live with me."

"Small condo near the police station. He'll have to get a job, fulfill the terms of his probation here, and he'll be well on his way," Vikkas replied.

"You asked them to give him his passport back immediately. And gave him money to live on for the moment since they took that fifty grand in counterfeit cash and the one hundred grand in real money." Confusion settled over him. "What's to keep him from leaving Durabia on the first thing smoking?"

Jai's smile was wider than the Durabian River and it totally matched Daron's as he said, "Not a damn thing."

* * *

Rahm stood on the sidewalk at the address Vikkas had sent him earlier. A vacant building sat smack in the middle of the Free Zone. He walked around the outside of the sleek structure. Overall, it wasn't a bad spot, but it could use a coat of paint. He just wasn't sure why Vikkas asked him to meet him here of all places.

The area was heavily populated with businesses, and he had spotted lots of tourists while he walked around. The habit of being aware of his surroundings at all times had never left him. He stopped moving as two cars approached. Once he realized the vehicles belonged to Vikkas and Sheikh Kamran, he relaxed his stance and waited on the men who had become his brothers.

"I see you found the place all right," Vikkas stated as he approached Rahm, pulling him into a brotherly hug.

Rahm stepped back, asking, "What's going on, guys? Why'd you ask me to meet you here?"

Sheikh Kamran spread his arms. "What do you think about this location?"

Rahm studied the building again. "It's fine, but I'm not sure why it would matter to me. It's not the one I picked."

"Actually, this is your building. I acquired it for you to start your tattoo business. The location of the other place is outside the Free Zone, too close to where nationals reside and would be tempted," Sheikh Kamran explained to a frowning Rahm.

"Was that the whole issue with me starting the business, the location?"

"It was, and I apologize for that. Do I need to search further?" Sheikh Kamran asked as he summoned his personal assistant, Waqas.

Rahm turned his back to both men for a few minutes to collect himself. Both men had concerned expressions when he turned around. He'd never been given anything in his life; it had always been about the hustle. "Are you serious?"

"It is yours, but there is a compromise or catch, as you say in America. You cannot ink *any* nationals," Sheikh Kamran warned. "However, they only make up ten to fifteen percent of the population. This shouldn't affect your bottom line too much."

"But I gave you a tattoo," he protested.

"That was different." Sheikh Kamran ran his fingers over the spot through his dishdasha. "That was a condition of my marriage."

"I get it," he said chuckling. "When do I sign the lease? When can I open for business?"

"First, calm down." Vikkas chuckled, handing him a sealed envelope.

Rahm opened it, clutched the document to his chest, and swayed on his feet. "Wait a minute! This is a deed. I can't accept this. I haven't paid for this." He shook his head. "As much as I appreciate the offer, this is not how I was raised. People don't give you anything without wanting something in return. I will sign a lease and make monthly payments." He handed back the envelope.

Vikkas pushed it down, and Sheikh Kamran placed one hand on Rahm's back. "Rahm, the hustle might have been your life, but you're a Knight of the Castle. I'm going to need you to work on being a cheerful receiver." He glanced at Sheikh Kamran who said, "Yes, a cheerful receiver. Even *I* can understand that, without translation."

Rahm gave him a side-eye.

"This is a *gift* to you from the Kings of the Castle," Vikkas said, putting the deed back in Rahm's hand. "Without help from you and Marilyn, Jai wouldn't still have his facility, not to mention the help you provided ridding the Castle of the vermin that resided there. Because of that, we all pitched in and purchased this place for you, so you can have a new start. Your other building can be used for something else."

"This is yours completely," Sheikh Kamran stated. "The deed has been registered, and your business license is in the works. By the time the place is painted and updated internally, it will be in your possession." He handed Rahm the key. "Now, let's go inside and check everything out."

They entered the building and did a walk-through, noting the repairs that needed to be made. Outside of minor wiring issues and the need for tables, tattoo benches, and chairs for his clients, the space would work just fine. As they exited the building, several trucks drove up, and the drivers approached Sheikh Kamran.

"These guys will paint the building today, and the electrician will have the wiring complete tonight as well," Sheikh Kamran said as he introduced the team to Rahm.

"Thanks, guys, this is wonderful." Rahm lifted both hands and let them fall. "I will forever be in your debt, and if you ever need anything, all you have to do is ask."

With a hand on Rahm's back, Vikkas said, "There is no need for repayment. This is brotherhood."

The vibrating of their phones stole the rest of their thoughts.

*"Cain has been taken into custody. Come to the airport immediately."*

The text was from Jai.

"Hop in, little brother," Vikkas yelled to Rahm as they piled into Sheikh Kamran's Rolls. The Sheikh could get away with breaking any speed limits.

\* \* \*

They arrived at the airport just in time to catch Cain being escorted from the police car.

"Jai, what's going on?" Rahm asked, as he rushed up to him.

"He tried to leave the country and was flagged at customs," Jai said. "The courts felt it was in the best interest to send him back to the United States for due processing since it was their counterfeit money."

*Courts my ass. This is Dro's doing.*

"Bro, come on; you have to help me," Cain pleaded, struggling against the constraints. "You know I can't go to prison. Tell them I did nothing wrong, please."

Rahm walked up to him and whispered, "I will help you just like you helped me." He stepped back as the officers pulled Cain away. They had to stand to the side as the passengers disembarked from the plane and came down the corridor.

His brother was screaming as he was escorted to meet his flight, but Rahm couldn't make out a word, nor did he care to. All the time he spent in Menard could've been avoided if Cain had just told what he saw. Told them about the weapon the man had. What would make a brother do that? He didn't have the wherewithal to care at the moment.

He glanced at the plane that had arrived minutes ago, in time to see a familiar figure descending the steps and leaning over the separating rail to pop Cain upside the head, causing the officers to laugh.

Rahm stood still as his body and soul told him the woman who meant more than life to him was on Durabian soil. Yet, he didn't fully believe. He whispered, "There is no way. That can't be ..."

Vikkas and Jai shared a grin as Rahm squinted at the plane to confirm what his spirit already told him.

"Marilyn?" Rahm shouted her name and hustled up the corridor. "What are you doing here? You said you didn't want this. Us."

Marilyn moved out of the path of the other passengers, rushing toward him with her arms outstretched. "I never said I didn't want you."

*Chapter 31*

"She's not dying," Alyssa said as her gaze moved from Ahmad to Lauren and back.

Lauren pressed the button to raise the hospital bed. "What do you mean?"

"As I said, she's not dying. The symptoms you described affected her but also affected your pet, right?" Alyssa asked.

"Yes," they both responded, shooting her a questioning glance.

"Have them test her for a bacterial disease called Leptospirosis. It's a relatively rare bacterial infection that affects people *and* animals. It can pass from animals to humans when an unhealed break in the skin comes in contact with water or soil where animal urine is present. Several species of the Leptospira genus of bacteria cause leptospirosis." She sighed, putting her focus on Ahmad. "Most times, this isn't detected until an autopsy."

"No. No more tests," Lauren pleaded. Her body was exhausted from all of the doctors' recent prodding.

Alyssa sat on the bed and took her hand. "Humor me, please. If not for yourself, then for your son. He deserves it."

After mulling that over for a moment, Lauren said, "All right."

"I wouldn't mention this if I didn't believe it's a possibility." Alyssa's gaze went to Ahmad, who stood at the door. "Are you all right?"

With a somber face, he said, "I've been bracing myself for her to transition, and I'm not sure if I want get up my hopes, or hers. Let's get Dr. Farquhar in here so he can make the call for those tests right away," he said, ringing for the nurse.

When she appeared to check Lauren's vitals, Ahmad gave the nurse instructions to call the doctor. Once she left the room, he continued his conversation with Alyssa. "Can you pass me my tablet? I want to read up on this. Figure out how all the doctors and specialists missed this. How I missed this."

Ahmad found some data and read from the screen. "… masked by the sclerodoma … hardening of the tissues or systemic sclerosis, is a chronic connective tissue disease generally classified as one of the autoimmune rheumatic diseases." Then he realized a further explanation was in order. "The word "scleroderma" comes from two Greek words: "sclero" meaning hard, and "derma" meaning skin. Hardening of the skin is one of the most visible manifestations of the disease.

Frowning, Ahmad focused on Alyssa. "How did you know?"

"I had to do extensive research on it for a novel I was writing," she answered. "I have a whole Banker's box of unique medical findings and treatments. When she mentioned that the dog also seemed ill around the same time and then became better when you gave him to your brother, it kind of clicked for me."

"The test is worth a try for Taj's sake," he said, taking Lauren's hand in his.

"I've been preparing to die for so long," Lauren whispered, her eyes wide with fear. "I don't think I'll know how to live."

"You'll figure it out." Alyssa patted Lauren's other hand, then leaned in, kissing Ahmad's cheek.

"Where are you going?" Ahmad asked as Alyssa grabbed her things from the chair near the window.

"Home," she replied. "I'm going home."

"Your home is with me." He walked with her to one corner of the room for some privacy.

"Not anymore, Lauren is on the mend. You will have your wife back now."

Ahmad gripped her upper arms to hold her in place. "Why are you always running away from something that's good for you?"

"Because I recognize when something is supposed to end," she said with a glance toward the bed.

"Who says it has to?" Ahmad asked.

"I do. Maybe what we've had is all we're supposed to have."

He laid his forehead against hers. "I don't believe that."

"So, you're going to abandon her to be with me?" She shook her head. "I don't think so."

"I want you, and I will still take care of her as I have been doing."

"Ahmad, that is *not* how this is going to work."

Alyssa walked out of the room with Ahmad right behind her. They went down the corridor into an alcove lined with comfortable seats. She faced him, brushing the hair off her face. "As a child, I watched my father cheat on my mother. I stood in the front of a store with a lollipop handed to me by my father before he took the owner to the back of the store. He bent her over a stack of pop and laid into her right out in the open. They thought I couldn't see, but mirrors were placed so the owner could see everything from the register. I hate lollipops to this day."

An elderly redhead walked inside and gathered her things from one of the chairs. When she left, Alyssa continued. "Open marriages don't work for me. No matter how you slice it, it's still cheating on some level. At the end of the day, I fear that all good love has an expiration date. It did with Tony, and now that time has come with you."

He gripped her arms and pulled her closer, pleading as he looked deep into her eyes. "You can't know, if you don't stay and try to work things through."

"I'm fine," she said. "We don't need to do that."

"Alyssa—"

"Stay with your wife, Ahmad." Her voice hitched, and she cleared her throat as she picked up the bag she had set down. "Ex-wife—the wife of your heart. You've been loyal to her all this time. No need for you to do anything different." She walked out of the alcove and down the hallway as the nurse rounded the corner and told him the doctor had arrived to see Lauren some minutes ago.

Ahmad hurried back, but the doctor swept past him on the way out. "We'll organize what needs to be done, Mr. Maharaj. This is awesome news. To think, a non-medical person may have figured this out."

"Thank you, Dr. Sudine," he said, wondering why they'd brought the head of oncology in on this case, instead of the attending physician.

Sitting up the moment he walked in, Lauren asked, "Where is Alyssa?"

"She's leaving," he said, feeling as if Alyssa had whacked him over the head, ripped his heart out, and taken it with her.

"Why?"

He let out his breath, suddenly exhausted, and looked her in the eyes. "So our marriage can resume."

"What marriage?" Lauren scoffed, shaking a fist in his direction. "Ahmad, you'd better go get that woman! Go to her before she does something foolish like cut you completely out of her life."

"But the doctor—"

"Will run the tests and do just fine without you. I'm in good hands." She made a shooing motion with her hands. "Go. Get. Your. Woman!"

Ahmad was conflicted, wanting to stay to be sure Lauren would be all right, but he also needed his woman. Lauren made another gesture for him to leave, and her heated glare said everything. "All right, I get it." He strode to the door and turned the handle. "I'll be right back."

"No, you won't. Take me out of the equation." Her smile was beautific when she said, "Make a life with her. You've been obligated to me, now become obligated to love. You've been a great man to me. Now be an even better man to her. I release you to have the love you deserve."

Ahmad hesitated, searching her eyes for some sign of deception, but there was none. A second later, he was out the door and striding toward the entrance.

# Chapter 32

Susan tucked the hair behind her ears as she paced the hotel room and waited for the call from Oliver. The plan was cut and dry. All he had to do was wait in the park near Ahmad's house. She gave him the key after they walked through the two plans several times. These days, Lauren slept deeply from the medication the doctors gave her. Taj always protested with the nanny when nap time rolled around, but he slept like the dead when he was tired.

*Ahmad could start again. Call it a retroactive abortion. Who'd be the wiser?*

More than once, Susan had stood over the sleeping boy who had been left unattended in his bedroom. The stuffed turtle sitting on his dresser would be sufficient.

Lauren would be just as easy. The grief would be exquisite, and just like with her last husband, Susan would be there to pick up the pieces. Surely Ahmad would see the sincerity and the dedication.

Married to him—a distant royal, meant she'd never have to return to the States, and even if she did they couldn't touch her. No one would dare. Diplomatic Immunity had a beautiful ring to it.

But the plan had failed. Security had become tighter at the house. Oliver told Susan that he'd seen Charli come out of the house one evening, and she laughed. The woman could barely sit up, so how on earth could she entertain anyone, but then she remembered the hospital visits where Lauren went in for treatment.

One hour, two, then three passed, and still no word.

"Oliver, just tell me. Yes or no," she shouted a message into her phone as she buffed her red lacquered nails on her jacket lapel.

Eighteen calls and still no word. Susan finally resorted to driving by his mansion. All the lights were on, as if a party was in full swing. When she rang the doorbell, the servant who answered the door staggered as Susan shoved it open.

She rushed up the spiral staircase and stumbled into his bedroom. "You know, all you had to do was give me a call to tell me it was finished. How selfish can you …"

The room still had the faint reek of urine from the water sports he played.

Her mouth filled with water as she eyed the pink furry handcuff still hanging from the ebony bed post. The vanilla-cream satin sheet was rumpled.

"Oliver, where are you? You were supposed to call me when it was done."

Susan crossed the floor and shoved the bathroom door open, expecting to see him on the toilet or in the jacuzzi. She dug into her linen jacket pocket for her phone, then sat on the edge of the tub.

Oliver was nowhere to be found.

She recalled the time she'd spent with him, in exchange for the job she wanted him to do. The first hour or so was spent with him pressing the button at the top of her thighs like a doorbell. The next involved him sucking and slurping at her the way he would a delicious bowl of soup. None of it mattered though. She endured his clumsy ministrations with her mind firmly fixed in the future.

Visions of Ahmad coming to her in tears to tell her of the accident that took his beloved ex-wife and son made Oliver's groans almost appealing.

For all Oliver's talk of how he was well endowed, the truth was revealed by a member that was no bigger than a thumb. The erection he brandished like a sword was due in no small part to the pump installed in one of his testicles, and he literally had to pump himself up like a bike tire. No wonder those private events appealed to him. Probably the only way he had the promise of laying that mini-pipe without having to pay for it—or walk away with whatever piece of self-esteem he had left.

Her phone buzzed in her hand, and she let out a yelp. "Where the fuck are you? Is it done? Did you do it?"

After a long silence Oliver answered, "It's done."

"You killed them? You *actually* killed them. It's finished? Lauren and her pesky pup are out of the picture?"

Susan stared at herself in the mirrored wall across from the tub, adjusting her clothes.

"I'll make a good wife," she whispered, her heart soaring with the anticipation of happiness. "Ahmad will see. It's a good match. We—"

She snatched the door open to find Oliver standing in the bedroom doorway, flanked by two police officers.

"Susan Abbott, or should we say Susan Maharaj, you are under arrest for the attempted murder of Lauren and Taj Maharaj."

The tallest officer moved forward with a pair of silver handcuffs dangling from one hand. Susan glanced at the pink furry cuff still attached to the bed post and then back at Oliver.

He stared back at her with red-rimmed eyes, and it all became too funny.

Susan giggled as if she had heard the best joke, but her laughter dissolved into blood-curdling screams.

# Chapter 33

"Rahm, I had time to think about things." Marilyn sighed and perched on the sofa. "My daughters are living their best lives now. Even Wanda has sought out therapy, trying to get her act together. Of course, it took her finally seeing Victor for what he was, and the fact that he cut her off." She shifted on the sofa, splaying her hand over the cushion. "I never wanted to walk away from you. There was so much going on at the time, and I couldn't think straight."

"And just like that, we're supposed to be fine?" Rahm had brought her home from the airport after folding her into his arms and practically lifting her off the floor. The Kings were taking turns caring for his mother to allow them this alone time. Brothers for real!

Now Rahm and Marilyn sat in his living room hashing things out.

"No, we're not," she shot back. "But we are two grown-ass people who never had trouble with words. I expect us to talk it out."

Rahm nodded but didn't move from his seat.

"Now you can sit there and pout like a little boy, or you can come over here and work this out like a grown man."

"Oh, it's like that?" Rahm closed the gap between him and Marilyn in one smooth step. "I missed you, woman."

Not one to mince words, Marilyn said, "Act like it then, man."

They discussed everything that transpired between them, which took a fair amount of time.

"I'm sorry for putting those ideas in your head about Victor and Wanda. It wasn't my place to interfere." He stroked her arm as he continued. "I also apologize for dumping my responsibilities in your lap. It was my job to handle my mom's Power of Attorney, and I shouldn't have tried to pressure you to come here."

Her facial expression changed several times during his confession, and Marilyn stopped his next sentence when she placed a finger on his mouth. "I accept your apology on the issue with your mother, but your suspicion about Victor and Wanda wasn't too far off."

"Damn," was Rahm's only reply as he pulled Marilyn into his arms.

"He didn't touch her, but he knew that his brother had several times. She was holding that over his head—and her uncle's. Collecting money from both. Instead of kicking his brother's ass as he should have, he chose to take it out on me." She shook her head. "I thought you missed me," she whispered. "Show me."

Rahm held her face as he kissed her tenderly on her eyes, nose, her forehead before moving to her lips. Once their tongues connected, a fire sparked, and the passion inside demanded its due. He slowly undressed her, peeling off her colorful wraparound dress and kissing his way down her body.

Marilyn's moans were a sexy, low purr that heated his blood. He continued his path and removed her boy cut panties one leg at a time. Once he completed that task, he knelt in front of her and paid tribute to her pearl.

Marilyn rubbed the back of his head, pulling him closer to the spot that needed his attention. Her love purrs grew louder, and his licks harder.

"I need more." Rahm spread her thighs and continued to feast on her body. He wanted her in the bed, but first, he had to provide her with this special moment—this release.

"Please don't stop," she moaned as her legs trembled.

Rahm flicked his tongue over her hard bud, and inserted two fingers inside her slick walls. That was all it took to release her savory nectar.

Marilyn's vocal level reached a new high, and Rahm was sure his neighbors would remember his name from now on.

He rose to his full height and led her to his bedroom. Making quick work of removing his clothes as she slowly traced the outline of his muscular frame and wrapped her hands around his erection. "Now, my turn."

"You don't have to do that," Rahm said. She had never tried this during their lovemaking before, and he had never pressured her to, either. "I appreciate the offer but ..." were the last words he said as she pushed him backward on the bed and her warm mouth closed around the head.

"*Fuuuuc ...*" He couldn't even finish the words as he clenched the sheets while she stroked him before taking him back into her mouth.

He watched her between half-closed eyelids and rested his other hand on the back of her neck. He didn't know when or where Marilyn learned this, but he definitely wasn't going to complain. "Baby slow down, or this is not going to last long."

"We have all night, and I'm just getting started. Let go." Marilyn relaxed her throat muscles and did something no other woman had *ever* done to him.

Rahm was sure the building shook as he released and howled her name.

He needed a few minutes to recover and cuddled her, stroking her hair as if he'd never let her go. Well, he had no plans on doing so.

As soon as they were both re-energized, they showered together, then he spent the rest of the night showing her how much she was missed and loved.

# Chapter 34

Alyssa couldn't see through the tears that blinded her. She would miss him, but faced the fact that the only reason Ahmad wanted her was because Lauren was dying. Since that was no longer the case, that meant no room was left in his life for her.

Lauren was all right with an open marriage scenario when she had no other choice. Now, probably not so much. And Ahmad was loyal to a fault. She thought Patti Austin and James Ingram serenading in the background was a sad reminder of what could have been. *Baby come to me ... let me put my arms around you ...*

Well, she would never feel those arms again.

A knock on the door snatched her attention. She had called for a bellman, but he should've arrived several minutes from now.

Who she found on the other side made her heart slam against her ribcage. Were they here with mischief in mind? She stood straight, keeping the lamp on the foyer table well within reach as she asked, "Why are you here?"

"We came to apologize for our actions," the trio answered.

"Understood," she said. "It's not necessary but appreciated."

"Just wanted to catch you before you left Durabia," Stewart stated. "Charli is holding a workshop for all of the remaining men today to open a discussion regarding consent and boundaries."

"Wow," she said, leaning against the door jamb. "And you're actually going? That's deep."

"Oliver won't be there," Gabe said with a look over his shoulder at Marc, who had been the quieter member of their little He-man crew. "I don't know if you heard, but he has some legal issues. Apparently, he was caught up in some murder-for-hire scheme.

"Talk about boundaries," Marc piped up, and Stewart stepped aside. "Seems someone tipped off the authorities to something they overhead in a bar. Who would be dumb enough to discuss those kinds of plans in public?"

Alyssa's left eyebrow shot up causing the three men to share a speaking glance.

"I have a question, if you don't mind," Alyssa said.

"Shoot," Gabe said, stuffing his hand into his slacks.

"You all obviously have money and lots of it."

Stewart chuckled and that boyish charm was on full display. "Don't mean to brag, but yes."

"Why on earth are you trolling a Bliss event for … whatever it is you're looking for?"

Gabe grimaced before replying, "Do you know how many marriages come out of those events?"

She shook her head.

"The ratio is extremely high. No jaded women, no games, no gold diggers, or money-hungry women. Just average, everyday people," Stewart said, with a grin. "The women are looking for something that can't be found anywhere else."

"And then you screw it all up by letting your dicks do the talking?" she snapped, her hand sliding up on her hips as she resisted the urge to smack each one of them upside the head. "How did you think that was going to go over with women?"

She let those words hang for minute, though she wasn't expecting an answer.

"Whew, look at the time. We have to get going," Stewart said, checking his watch before he turned to leave.

"What are you doing here?" Ahmad roared from behind the group. Within a blink he dragged Stewart past them, kicking and screaming toward the glass doors leading to the balcony.

"Didn't I warn you about her?"

"Ahmad, No," Alyssa screamed. She rushed to catch up with him while Stewart's friends stood gawking, then finally caught a clue and ran behind her.

Ahmad faced her, keeping Stewart in his tight grip. One wrong move and he would meet his maker a lot sooner than he intended.

"They came to apologize—nothing more. They were leaving. I promise you," she said, rushing her words.

Ahmad's chest heaved as he listened to her explanation, but it did not seem to register.

"Ahmad, please. Please, honey," she begged him. "Don't kill him. We need you here, not on the wrong side of twenty-five to life."

The moment he was free, Stewart did a one-hundred-meter dash toward the door and zoomed past his friends and the bellman whose panic-stricken expression spoke volumes. Gabe and Marc flickered a gaze at Ahmad who tilted his head and glared at them. Soon they overcame their struggles to get their bearings and were out the door.

She signaled for the bellman to take the tip envelope next to the lamp and make an exit. He didn't have to be told twice.

With both hands propped on her hips, Alyssa chided him, "Ahmad, you can't kill people for simply being in my presence."

"The hell you say," he roared. "It was three to one. They could have—"

"They stayed on the other side of the threshold," she reasoned. "And Rahm sent Cameron Stone to teach me some self-defense techniques. Not to mention, I'm from the southside of Chicago, honey. I can throw a punch and take a punch."

He caught his breath and moved closer but kept a few feet between them. "Well, from where I saw it …"

"The bigger question is, why are *you* here?" She closed the door and placed her back against it.

Ahmad approached her, then said, "To reclaim what's mine."

*Why do those words sound so amazing?* "I am no longer needed," she said, avoiding that intense look in his dark, piercing eyes. "I am no longer yours, Ahmad."

"Says who?" He stretched out a hand but didn't touch her. "Not once did those words cross my lips."

Alyssa hid her pain and forced the words from her lips. "Lauren is going to live. She is going to be fine. Life, as you know it, can resume."

"That would have been true if I had never met you."

"And why aren't you at the hospital with your wife?"

"*Ex*-wife," he corrected. "*Ex*. And I swear to you, that woman was about to get out of that bed and kick my ass if I didn't come for you. And you would have been next on her list. I have never seen Lauren that angry before in my entire life."

She absorbed the permission Lauren had given in that selfless act, but put her hand up to keep him at bay. "Ahmad, enough. What we had was temporary. Truly. You need someone by your side who can paint the right picture for your lifestyle."

"What the hell is that supposed to mean?" he fumed.

"What we had was for a time," she said in a low tone, trying not to let his presence affect her as much as it did. "You need someone who—"

"Honey, you are part of all of that." He stroked a hand across her shoulders, down her arms, brought it onto her belly, then around her waist before traveling to her back and bringing her closer to him. "And I love that about you. I love it, but I am *in love* with you. There is no comparison. You submitted to me. Said you were mine, and now you want to flip the script."

Alyssa gave him a dismissive wave. "Those things were said in the heat of passion. They don't carry any weight."

"Says who?" He smiled and wrapped her voluptuous frame in his arms. "Woman, where are you getting your flawed logic from?"

"My past relationships before Tony showed that once men get what they want, they are no longer invested in a relationship. They want the cookie, but not the crumbs. And the crumbs are where all the pain is situated. The crumbs are the pieces that have fallen off and sometimes get swept from the floor."

"We aren't talking about anyone but me," he countered. "I can't believe you place such little value on what we have."

His words struck her right in the heart, but she didn't defend herself. He was breaking her down by the second.

"I want you. *All* of you. I desire the whole, everything—cookies, crumbs, packaging with whatever label, and the ingredients etched on the back." Ahmad brushed his lips across hers and her knees nearly gave out. She wanted him just that bad. Never knew that heartbreak could be a physical thing.

"Tasting a cookie once is what *boys* do. A real man wants to learn the ingredients that make the treat delectable. He wants to savor the goodness for life." Ahmad held her face in his hands, and she pulled away. The flash of pain in his eyes brought tears to her own.

"Great, then you tell me how." He leaned against the wall with his arms folded.

Alyssa made her way into the living room, trying to put some distance between them. As she swept past, she said, "Excuse me?"

Ahmad followed her, and when she faced him, his gaze was fixed on her suitcases near the door. His lips twisted when his focus went to the flight itinerary on the coffee table. As he tore his gaze from the blue airline folder and met her eyes, his expression became crestfallen.

"Seems to me you had no problems walking away from me. Show me how it's done." He tilted his head as if daring her. "You seem to have no problem whatsoever."

"You think it was easy," Alyssa shot back. "Every step was like a knife in me." She inched closer, then thought better of it. "It was the best choice for all involved. There was nothing easy about any of this."

"Evidently it was all too easy," he said in a voice just above a whisper. "The minute you saw an escape, you turned your back on me;

turned your back on us."

His gaze accused her, but the pain and the shadows in his eyes made her heart ache all over again.

"This is ridiculous. I'm giving you your freedom," she protested. "Most men would jump at the chance." Alyssa folded a stray blanket, placed it on the back of the sofa, and moved to the fully stocked kitchen aiming for some liquid courage to warm the parts of her that hurt.

Ahmad rounded her so quickly with a hand on her arm that she bumped into him. "I am *not* most men. I am the one who sees the tears beneath your calm exterior and would gladly spend the rest of my life loving them away." His voice lowered to a tone that was so filled with emotion she could barely breathe. "Show me how, Alyssa. Show me how to live without you."

"Ahmad ..." A sharp pain pierced her heart, as if he'd squeezed it in a vice and left it shattered. Alyssa wiped absently her face, hoping her tears wouldn't fall and betray her.

"I can exist, but that is all it would be. Existing." He lowered his head. "If you ask it of me, I will go. I will respect your boundaries. But please, before I do, show me how to live without you."

Ahmad walked away but paused when he reached the door. "You know, it's funny I've been asking for permission to give you so many things. Should have been more mindful of my heart." He shook his head. "Doesn't matter. It's yours anyway."

He snatched the door open, but she couldn't let him leave. Not this way. Not after showing her what was in his heart. Never had a man been this vulnerable with her.

"Ahmad, wait."

At her request, he released the handle and pressed his forehead against one of the panels.

Alyssa laid a hand between his shoulder blades, feeling his muscles ripple under her touch.

"I can't show you how, Ahmad ..."

He turned and put his back against the door.

"I've been living half a life since I—"

The last of her words were lost in a deep, toe-curling kiss. A breathless whimper escaped her as he swept an arm under her thighs and carried her to the bedroom. Their tongues danced as they melted against each other. He released her legs and let her slide down the front of his body. She embraced him as moisture flowed from her core, ready to welcome him.

As they lay next to each other, every layer he peeled away from her was replaced with warm, wet trails of sensuous kisses that seared with every touch.

She tugged at his clothing and flicked at the side of his neck, writing her name in his skin.

When she was wantonly naked beneath him, Ahmad slowly journeyed to her treasure line and lower still, until at last, he found her jewel.

As his tongue dipped between the silken, glistening seam of her lips, Alyssa arched her back. Her palms skimmed across his neck and muscular shoulders, then she clung to him and angled her hips under his.

Ahmad ran his fingernails up her sides as if telegraphing his intentions into her quivering skin. Only then did he lower his head to tease her nipples.

She clutched at his hips as Ahmad scored her with the molten-hot hardness of his arousal. Her moans offered him permission to seal their union, but he held back. Her eyes flicked open to meet his, but he smiled then spoke next to her ear. "This moment is all about you. Never again will you know darkness, or fear, or pain. Never again will your hunger be denied. This moment, this sacred bond, is only the beginning. My passion for you is unending. When I'm finished with you, there will never be a moment when any of your desires are left untapped or unmatched."

She gasped as tears of joy trickled across her cheeks. "Yes, Ahmad. I'm for every bit of that."

Alyssa gripped his hips and settled under him.

The moment he sank into the rich cleft between her thighs, she whispered, "Come inside me, Ahmad. Make me yours."

He pulled away for a few seconds to look into her eyes, then asked, "Permission to love you for the rest of your life?"

The certainty in his voice brushed aside any remaining doubt of who she belonged to, and Alyssa drew him to her breasts, whispering, "Permission granted."

# Chapter 35

Everyone had left the plane after it landed in the States, except Cain, who remained handcuffed to the chair. The FBI agents entered as he was trying to pry the seat loose.

"Going somewhere?" The red-haired agent questioned.

"No, sir," Cain responded, sitting up straight. "My arms were just getting tired, and I need to use the restroom."

They escorted him to the bathroom and stood with the door open.

"Can I get some privacy," Cain asked, his eyes darting between the agent that uncuffed him and the brown-haired one who kept his hand on his gun. "You can take your hand off the weapon. I'm not trying to get shot in the back or anywhere else."

"You should get used to no privacy. There will be very little where you're going," the brown-haired agent stated.

Cain washed his hands the best he could and dried them on his pants. "Why am I being arrested here?" He asked. "Don't I get to see your badges?"

Both men pulled out their badges, and he read their names out loud, "Agent Ross and Agent Timms.

"You broke into a house owned by Daron Kincaid," Agent Ross, the red-haired agent responded.

"You don't have any proof of that." Cain searched both of their expressionless faces wondering how they knew anything about that. He had scoped out the house and doubled back to collect more cash. He was well aware that Daron had been too preoccupied with a phone call to coordinate their new flight times to reset the alarms on the way out. That's when he made a choice to strike then before that miniature Fort Knox was locked up tight.

Agent Timms grabbed him by the arm and proceeded to the door to disembark, reading him his rights as they went. "Actually, we have a whole video of you and four others entering the house and leaving with a bag. One of them was a Melvin Olgetree, Dipping, who was just released from Menard. We also have footage of the room where the two of you went under the safe and removed the cash. So, try again."

"Damn, I think I need a lawyer." Cain felt the wind had been knocked out of him.

"A public defender will be appointed to you once you are arraigned tomorrow morning."

Cain put his head down as they continued through the airport, avoiding the curious glances coming their way. The two agents rushed him into the car that waited. "Can I call my brother?" He asked.

Agent Ross responded, "You are allowed one call, but that won't happen until after you're processed."

Timms started the car and drove off, headed to the nearest precinct. Cain stared out of the window, praying that Rahm would take his phone call when he was finally allowed to make one.

Thirty minutes later, they arrived at a beige brick building with a serious hustle and bustle of activity, where he was hauled in to be processed.

"Put this on," the burly officer said, pushing the standard-issue orange jumpsuit his way. "Take off your shoes and put these loafers on." After that, he was fingerprinted and placed in an empty room.

When the two agents from earlier entered the room, he immediately asked, "My phone call, please? My brother's still in the place I just left."

"It's four in the evening here, and one in the morning there, so you will need to wait until around ten or later here to call. We wouldn't want to start an international incident calling royalty at ungodly hours," Agent Timms stated with a grin.

"What, royalty? I'm talking about my brother. He ain't royalty," Cain shot back.

Agent Timms sat at the table and opened the folder, "Let's go over your charges. Maybe we can cut you a deal if you give us the names of the others."

"I told you I didn't do anything, and I'm not speaking about it until I talk to my brother, and I have a lawyer present."

"Fine, suit yourself," Timms said, placing his papers back in the folder. "Rest up."

They tapped the door, and the officer escorted Cain to a cell. On the way, he passed two of his guys who lowered their heads. Dippin' glared openly at him, then came forward to say, "You set me up, you bitch. Wait 'til we're inside. Your ass is mine. Literally."

For a minute, fear struck in his heart, but then he remembered, he wouldn't have to see any of those dudes again. They had him on counterfeit charges which would land them in Federal prison, a virtual club compared to a State prison. Easy time. No worries. They had them on breaking and entering. State time. A hard knock life.

Right now, he just needed to stay awake to speak with Rahm and get this all sorted out.

\* \* \*

"Fosten, wake up," the burly officer said. "Let's go; it's time for court.

Cain rubbed the sleep from his eyes. "What do you mean? I was supposed to receive a phone call," he asked as he slid his feet in his shoes and walked toward the bars.

"I guess you overslept. The night clerk said he tried to wake you, but you wouldn't get up."

"Man, that's some bull. No one tried to wake me up," he responded. "I don't sleep that hard. What kind of games are you guys playing?"

He escorted Cain to the van, and they drove the few blocks to the courthouse. As soon as they arrived, he was ushered in line with the others into the holding area.

"Cain Fosten?" A little guy with a stack of folders that nearly dwarfed him, called out.

"Yes, that's me," he responded, still pissed that they hadn't allowed him the call that would have settled this. His brother had major pull around these parts. He wasn't sleeping that damn hard.

"I'm Ernie Tate, your public defender," he said over the noise in the courtroom. "The district attorney is going to go hard on you because you're connected. You could land a deal by turning on the others who did the crime with you."

"I'm no snitch," Cain snarled, glancing over his shoulder. "You heard what happens to those."

"Then after judge gives you bail, we fight, but my suggestion is that you plead guilty and get a lesser sentence." He moved forward, allowing another attorney in a tight little pencil skirt to shimmy past. "You have a clean record, that's going to factor into things. How did you even come in contact with someone like Melvin Ogletree?"

"See, the thing is," Cain said, leaning in to whisper. "He was looking for my brother. Had a score to settle so we came to an arrangement. He slid a lot of dollars my way so I would find a way to get Rahm back in the States. When I didn't come through at the time Dippin' wanted, he asked for the money back, but it was gone. The only chance I had to pay him back was when dude went in the house and had all that money laying around. He wouldn't miss it. Dude was rolling in it."

"You paired up with your brother's enemy?" Ernie asked, his expression was nothing short of shocked.

"You know what they say," Cain said with a grin. "The enemy of my enemy is my friend."

"That's cold." Ernie let out a breath. "Glad you're not my family."

The bailiff took his place at the front of the courtroom, signaling that it was time for the proceedings to start.

"They have a video, and all it will take is the right deal for your boys to say that it was your idea," he said as the conversation died down. "Unless you're going to serve them up and cut a deal, do yourself a favor and say you're guilty."

"If that's how you're rolling, then I'll defend myself. I'm not going to jail. Like you said, my brother's got connections. I'm using that."

The guard escorted him back to the benches where all the prisoners were situated.

Cain waited through all the other cases. This judge was not playing. He sent one guy to jail for four days for not removing his son from the courtroom due to the nature of the hearings. He didn't even care that he was taking his son to the doctor.

"Next case please," the judge said once he had the child situated in his chambers.

"Cain Fosten," the bailiff called as Cain was brought to the defendant's table and stood alone.

"Where's your attorney?"

"I'm here," Ernie said taking his space by Cain's side.

"I just fired him. Fool wanted me to roll over and play dead. That's not happening."

The judge looked down the rim of his glasses. "You know who else is considered a fool?"

Cain shrugged as Ernie took a few steps to distance himself.

"Excuse me," the judge said.

"No, why don't you clue me in, Your Honor."

"A man who represents himself has a fool for a client," the judge answered.

"Simple case," Cain countered. "Counterfeit money. Do a little club fed time."

"Really," the judge shot back with a smile. "Carry on."

The assistant district attorney laid out the charges.

"Mr. Fosten, how do you plead?" The judge asked.

The courtroom quieted as everyone awaited the response. Fear of receiving a lengthy sentence spiked in those who veteran criminals; as well as those with much cleaner records who were facing the same judge. Cain wasn't one of them. He knew he was a first-timer, and they would go easy on him.

"Not guilty, Your Honor," Cain responded.

"Your Honor, we have enough evidence to hold him over for trial, but due process and all," the DA stated, looking directly at Cain. "He has substantial ties in the Middle East, a very powerful family with private jets and can go into hiding."

*Damn, Rahm has moved up in the world.*

"We ask that he be required to surrender his passport, and post bail of three million." He shifted his gaze to Cain. "And we'll take real cash, thank you very much."

"No objection," Cain said, leaning over to Ernie who was paying more attention to the judge's clerk than to what was happening with his case.

"You fired me, remember," he shot back, taunting, "You're on your own … my brother."

"I have read the charges, took the assistant district attorney's recommendation under advisement. Based on that, Mr. Fosten, you will be the guest of Cook County Jail until your trial. Do you have anything you would like to say to the court?"

"I never got my phone call," Cain grumbled. "That is not due process."

"They'll make sure you get a phone call once you're booked," the judge replied, gesturing for the bailiff to come close. "I see a long future for you in your final place of residence."

"Club Fed," Cain said with a relieved sigh.

"Menard," the judge corrected, causing Cain's hopes to sink. "The breaking and entering charge takes a front seat to any monopoly money. If you're convicted, State is going to take a bite first, then you'll visit Club Fed. And because I'm so generous, we're going to fast track your case."

For the first time, Fear hit right in the center of his soul.

The public defender he had fired leaned over and whispered, "The Kings and Knights of the Castle send their regards."

# Chapter 36

*Desperation has a smell.*

The smell coated the surfaces of Susan's surroundings; multiplying in the cleaning solvent she used to mop the floors. The aroma, like the stench of urine, lived in the orange jumpsuits Susan laundered during duty rotation.

Privacy was a myth. Peace was a rumor, and time was an endless elastic band, long past its prime. The trial had been as swift as the punishment.

Apparently, attempting or even conspiring to kill a Royal in Durabia was taken very seriously. They couldn't or wouldn't understand that she was under insurmountable stress. She wasn't thinking clearly. Temporary insanity. Yes, that's what it was. Her heart was broken. Call it a crime of passion, but she certainly wasn't responsible for any of her actions.

Oliver had played his role, but a plea deal whisked him away to the States with a slap on the wrist, loss of his financial holdings and property in Durabia, and a warning never to return. She on the other hand, wanted to be handed over to the American authorities who had indicted her for an extensive number of crimes. There, her father had an extensive amount of pull.

"Hurry up, Suzie, I got the bubble guts!" Teresa "Recey" Gibbons whined. The woman was in for espionage and was awaiting extradition back to the States.

Seemed like everyone was headed back to the good old US of A except her. She got her wish to remain out of the clutches of American courts, but not quite how she wanted it. Susan smiled at the irony.

Recey inched closer to Susan, who was on her hands and knees finishing the last stall in the women's detention facility. "Unless you wanna watch." She snickered, but Susan found nothing funny. "You look like the type that watches while others get their hands dirty. Yeah, how them nails doin?" she mocked as she leaned over Susan's shoulder. "You gotta new kinda manicure. Not so pretty sopping up all kinds of waste now, huh? Don't know where those gloves could have gone to. Sorry, sis."

Susan's stomach threatened to send back her morning meal. She lifted one of her raw, red hands. The crimson bombshell nail lacquer she wore was long gone. Split cuticles framed nails bitten to the quick. She stood, grabbing the scrub bucket as Recey pushed her aside and slammed the door to the stall.

The logic made sense when she was in the midst of planning. After sitting a spell in central booking, the flaws blossomed like dandelions in her mind. The slam of cell doors sounded in Susan's bones, much like the gavel when the judge rendered his decision. The crimes against the people and their beloved royal family demanded the maximum punishment. Everyone said that Durabian prison was better than any American one—hands down.

Requests for appeals were filed and denied because she was a flight risk. Which was funny, because where could she really go? From frying pan to the fire, the fall was just as far. And wouldn't you know it, a long distance from all the people she had made rich; all the ones she did favors for, were unable to come to the phone or they were permanently elsewhere.

Saltwater filled her mouth at the memory of the payment arrangement for a private call with the burner phone hidden in her cellmate, Ruby Blue's left prison-issued moccasin. A turn with one of the screws meant

Susan acquired a package of anti-depressants and Oxies. Of course, they were for a well-documented case of clinical depression and anything else the last of her slush fund could buy.

Susan stuck her hands under the hard-hot water at the sink. The polished steel that passed for mirrors beckoned her gaze. When she first arrived, she had preened. Lessons in humility, courtesy of Ruby Blue, made short work of the thousands Susan spent on caps and veneers. As Susan's diet changed to such inferior drivel, so did her reflection.

All the malice, insecurity, and fear she thrived on found a safe place to hide beneath her skin. The pounds she had gained were better than a lover. They were soft, and suffocating, and everything she feared—such steadfast loyalty choking out everything good and clean and privileged in her life. The one visitor she had, came in the form of Chaz, her ex-husband, or so she thought.

*Scanning the family members smiling and talking to the other inmates made her nervous. Susan sat at the table picking at the material of her orange jumpsuit. Crossing her legs became cumbersome as her thighs thickened. Which according to Ruby Blue, would make great earmuffs when she stopped being so uppity.*

*Susan could almost see her cellmate's dark-brown buzz cut hair. Ruby enjoyed making Susan cringe by running her ulcered tongue over cracked lips before flashing a smile with those tobacco stained, gold-capped teeth.*

Still, Susan tried to make herself smaller and pathetic in her chair. Maybe if she turned on the tears, Chaz would remember how they were in the past, and whisk her from this place. She might even give him the whelp he wanted as a tribute. Yeah, she could do that with enough nannies and house staff.

"I knew you'd come." She flipped her greasy hair back from her face and faced forward in her chair.

Mandy slid into the seat across from her and folded her arms. Susan searched the area around Mandy as she sat back. When she realized Chaz wasn't coming, she settled her gaze on the woman she'd done a little damage to eons ago.

"I guess you're here to rub my face in it and smack my ass like a bad dog, huh?"

Mandy was beautiful. The purple silk tunic she wore flowed over her skin like water. Her French manicured hands were now folded neatly on the table as her dark eyes radiated pain and pity.

Susan glanced to her left at a woman sobbing silently into her hands as a tall, gaunt man looked on with scorn and a hint of disgust.

"I've placed money on the books for you, Susan. For anything you may need."

Susan squared her shoulders at that insult. "Take it off. I don't want anything from you."

"Chaz said you'd say as much. I told him he was wrong." Mandy shifted in her chair, but her gaze never left Susan's face.

"Well, there you go." Susan moved to stand, and felt the warmth of Mandy's hand on hers. She wrinkled her nose and snatched away. "I don't regret it, you know."

Mandy shook her head in confusion, or it might have been pity. Susan waved her chapped hand as if to silence her before she could inquire into the meaning behind those words.

"Anything I did was a small pittance. You owed me. You stole my life," she sneered and she sat straight. "So, if you came here asking for forgiveness ..."

"Hardly. I have forgiven you, though. I release you to live and be happy. Just like I am with my husband and children. A life you nearly stole from me by putting me in prison just weeks after my children were born." Mandy chuckled as she stood. "That was some low down dirty mess right there. But God had other plans. Won't He do it?"

"Oh, so you're doing the Christ-like thing? Spare me. You're a phony," Susan roared as she stood and kicked her chair out of the way.

The guards swarmed around her and escorted Mandy to safety.

Susan blinked away the memory and forced herself to look at her muted reflection. Susan came from old school money, but her father washed his hands of her with this arrest that stained the family's image. Coupled with the fact that he no longer had the same power he once held, since most of the Mississippi judges that were once in his pocket were now serving time themselves.

She smiled, exposing the darkened pegs of her implants, and slipped her brunette hair, with the last remnants of blonde highlights, behind her ear. She smoothed her hands over the acne scars and the active blemishes, before tracing the rolls of flesh that hung from her face in double chins.

For an instant, the world fell away. She was transported back in her luxury hotel room staring at her reflection with the sun pouring in past the double doors. The scent of spices perfumed the wind, making the white curtains leading out to her balcony billow. A mantra came to her as she studied her flawless skin with the crystal chandelier behind her catching the morning light.

*I am a beautiful flower basking in the light. I am the light, and the light is within me.*

The toilet flushing three times in rapid succession snapped Susan back to reality. Hints of the sour remains of Recey's meal flooded the air. Susan raked a hand through her hair. The faint tendrils of a day's sweat, now rancid, reached her nose. She made a mental note to scrub extra hard that evening to rid herself of the smell.

From somewhere in the hallway, Susan caught the first notes of an old nursery rhyme as the hair stood on the back of her neck. Every night since her arrival, the same measure of music—carried on stale cigarette-tainted breath—from one cell to another until at last Ruby Blue began to hum through a close-lipped smile before whistling through her gapped teeth.

Recey picked up the melody and whistled. One whistle became two, then three, and more. Susan's bladder let go first, and then her bowels, just as rank and fetid as Recey's.

*Fear also has a smell.*

The woman stopped whistling and ambled closer. "Did you forget what today is?" Recey asked in that gravelly voice Susan had come to hate.

"I told you I didn't have any money," she snapped. "That supply of medication was a one off. It took everything I had."

"The guards heard that rich chick tell you that she put a lot of money on your books. So, you got something. And you can get more."

Without turning to look at the woman, Susan ran her pinky over her bottom lip. "You're a bunch of leeches. Well, there's nothing left. And even if there was, I wouldn't give it to you free-loading bitch hogs. You can go tell—"

The words died in her throat.

Susan watched as Recey's reflection was joined by others. Some were taller than others. Each woman took a space around her. The whistling ceased, and the humming began. Always the same sick lullaby.

Recey bumped her with a hip to make Susan turn around.

"Now come on, sis. You know Ruby Blue don't like messy accounts. She'll get her pound of flesh. One way or the other. We all do," Recey warned as her eyes drifted past Susan. "From the looks of you, you've got plenty to spare."

Out of the corner of her eye, Susan saw the reflection of the doorway darken, and she raised her crystal-blue gaze to the ceiling.

Ruby's ivory-white hand swept from left to right, opening Susan's throat.

She reached for the stinging, gaping wound as the first of many shivs punctured places all over her body.

As her eyes fluttered shut and Susan heard the blood raining down on the floor in soft patters, fear and desperation gave way to relief.

*Someone else will have to clean the bathrooms tonight.*

# *Chapter 37*

Alyssa sat on the patio of her home overlooking the Durabian River, writing her next novel. Now a *New York Times* Bestselling Author, thanks to a dynamic marketing team Ahmad had put in place to promote *Love is Bliss*, a romance that chronicled her journey into finding herself, then love.

She spent most of her afternoons writing. Her mornings were spent teaching children like Taj to read. The ones professionals had cast away as hard to educate or labeled as ADHD. The ones that caused teachers to be riddled with more paperwork than they could handle while trying to force the same type of education into children in the traditional way. When all they needed was someone patient enough to sit down and relate to the way they learned.

She watched Ahmad playing with Taj in the pool, over the top of her shades. "Yes," she whispered, forgetting she wasn't alone until she heard Lauren chuckle beside her.

"What?" rolled off her tongue. She barely contained her laugh at her friend, who had stretched out on the lounge chair next to her.

"I only chuckled at your inability to hide your lust for him. But I guess it's not lusting if he belongs to you, right?" Lauren replied.

"Honey, it's still lust," she admitted. "Even though he's mine, there are days when I can't believe everything that transpired. Who would've thought this would be my life." She gestured toward their new home that was situated on an estate with a view of the Durabian skyline.

"I understand the feeling," Lauren said, her eyes sparkling. "Remember, at this point, I thought I would be dead, and that crazy Susan would be raising my child. I'm so grateful you entered our lives when you did. Because of you, I have a new lease on life, a new spouse, and I get to watch my son grow up happy." She grabbed Alyssa's hand. "So thank you for everything. I can never repay you what I owe you, but you have my friendship and loyalty for life."

Both shared a moment of reflection before the splash of the water and small feet padding against the ground caught their attention.

"Taj, no running around the pool," came Ahmad's stern voice. "We've discussed this several times, young man."

"Yes, Papa." Taj came to a halt before he hugged and kissed his mother then Alyssa.

"Go shower and change," Ahmad said to a retreating Taj as he made his way inside the house.

"If you keep that up, we'll need to send our guest home." Alyssa said in response to the kisses Ahmad trailed down her neck.

The longing in his eyes fueled her need as he traced the length of her body with his gaze. A huge smile came to his face as he said, "We have all night to satisfy each other, my love." He kissed Alyssa and then pecked Lauren on the forehead. "Good to see you."

"Same here," Lauren said, to his retreating frame.

"So how are things between you and Charli," Alyssa questioned.

"It's wonderful," Lauren responded, practically beaming. "I couldn't ask for a more loving and supportive partner."

"Wait, are you blushing?" Alyssa asked, reaching out to touch her friend's cheek that had turned crimson. "That's so sweet. I just want your happiness. You sacrificed a lot for me to be here."

"Please, I gave up nothing," Lauren said, waving the thought away. "Ahmad and I were over long before you came. He only stayed because he's a good man; a loyal man. But Charli came here one night to check on you after some trouble at the Bliss party. We ended up talking until morning and the majority of the day after."

Ahmad brought them a pitcher of sweet tea, placed it and four glasses on the table between them and kept moving toward the pool where he did a cannonball that brought peals of laughter from Taj who had somehow convinced Ahmad for a little more pool time.

"It's like she opened the pages of my soul and read every line," Lauren said, looking down at the pages of the book in her hand. "Here I was, ready to die and she asked for permission to love me for however much time I had left. When I told her about my diagnosis, that I would live, I asked her if she could love me for the rest of my life. She said, 'No, but I will love you for the rest of mine and I'm not going any damn where without you.'"

Alyssa sighed. Those words were close to the ones that Ahmad had spoken to her.

"Well, I knew she was my soulmate and the love of my life."

Alyssa placed her laptop on the table and glanced at her friend, "Who would've thought that a chance meeting would end with you two falling in love?"

"I could say the same for you an Ahmad," Lauren teased.

Charli and Lauren had spent a lot of time together and Lauren ventured into the Bliss workshops to see how Charli was working with men to understand boundaries and consent. Between the workshops and the actual Bliss events, they discovered a lot of commonalities and became close. As Ahmad and Alyssa worked on their new relationship, she was able to work on hers as well. Once Lauren was sure that her recovery was certain, they announced their budding relationship to everyone. They married a few weeks after Ahmad and Alyssa said their nuptials.

"I'm just glad Ahmad built these houses in a way that we could be neighbors." Alyssa refilled their glasses with tea and handed one to Lauren. "Now Taj has the benefit of being close to both parents. What a wonderful way this all turned out."

"I'm happy that my son has you as a mother as well." Lauren took a few sips of her tea and set the glass on the table beside Alyssa's before beckoning Taj to come to her. "And on that note, I'll take Taj home with me so you two can have some alone time," Lauren stated, walking to the door just as the bell chimed. "Oh, and whatever you do to him that makes him howl like that, I need the notes."

Alyssa threw back her head and laughed. "You better watch out. Next thing you know, I'll be writing a manual."

Rahm and Marilyn slid out of the glass patio doors with a guest and two children in tow. The woman was beautiful, had features that seemed vaguely familiar. Alyssa stood, as her mind filtered through the possibilities of who this woman might be. She'd met both of Marilyn's daughters, so she couldn't be one of them.

"Rahm, who—"

"Auntie, you always had something to say about the Kings, but they serve their purpose." His smile widened as he brought the woman to his side. "They have a network that reaches all over the globe."

Alyssa couldn't take her eyes off the young woman, and heart rate increased.

"Mommy, is that grandma," the little boy asked, looking directly at Alyssa whose heart began to pound so hard she could barely hear anything else.

"Rahm …Rahm … Rahm," Alyssa whispered trying to rein in her emotions. Ahmad was by her side, bracing her right at the moment her knees nearly gave out.

"They find lost loved ones, too," Rahm said with a smile and a nod in Ahmad's direction. "Cousins, daughters, you know … family."

Alyssa broke away from Ahmad and rushed to her daughter, enveloping her into an embrace before breaking into sobs that ripped through her body. She couldn't speak. She couldn't think.

"Mama," Shayna whispered, tears streaming down her face as her two little ones leaned in and tried to wrap their arms around both of them, trying to edge in for their own hug. They stayed that way for nearly an eternity.

"Lauren, Taj, don't leave," Alyssa called out, catching them before they crossed the threshold. "I'd like you to meet the rest of my family."

# Chapter 38

Rahm's business was booming. Between the tourists and all of the locals who wanted tattoos, he had grossed more in his first year here than he was making in Chicago. He was so grateful that Sheikh Kamran had hooked him up with state-of-the-art equipment. And he had found a way to deal with the nationals who had tried to sneak in and get one done. He was not losing his license and business for anyone.

The struggle to get his mother's Power of Attorney was behind him, and she was in Durabia under a doctor's care, and with "companions", women her age that kept a tight watch on her and provided some friendship; so he had no worries on that score.

He continued to ink the young man on his table. The blond curls flowed freely over the bench, unlike his eyes that he held clenched tight. A little dramatic for all the tough guy image he presented. Tattoos felt like a few little pinpricks, like when someone had an allergy test. After the first ones, people adjusted and the rest of the sessions always went smoothly.

"I'm almost done, sir. About five more minutes. I just have to add the color in the 'Y' of Ruby. Who is she?" Rahm asked.

"She's my mother," the youngster responded. "That's the only woman who will love me all my life, regardless of how far I fall. I know I can always go home."

"That's true, and when she can't take care of herself, make sure you're there for her. The same way she was for you." He finished the blue color fill-in of the name, which was the same as his eyes. "All done."

Rahm provided care instructions and walked him to the register.

"That wasn't so bad, was it?" Marilyn asked from behind the desk with a smile on her face.

"No, ma'am, it wasn't bad at all," he said with a glance at Rahm before they both shared a laugh. "I handled it like a champ."

Rahm maneuvered around the desk and placed a kiss on Marilyn's cheek. He watched as she returned his client's card and bid him farewell.

Rahm took her in his arms, "Hey, wife," he said, rubbing her belly. "How are you feeling today?"

"I feel wonderful," She placed her hand on his. "The doctor said the baby was doing well. I had heard of women getting pregnant during menopause, but never in a million years would I have that thought that would be my fate."

"It was your decision to skip the condoms on our wedding night. I tried my best to convince you," Rahm laughed.

She patted his hand before moving it. "You sure did. How would I know that everything was still in working order."

"Damn straight it is," he said nuzzling her neck.

Marilyn joined him in laughter. Rahm held her hand again as they walked over to the station, where he cleaned up from his last appointment. "How about I finish this up, and we go home? You can take a nice, long bath, I'll cook dinner, and when we finish maybe I can rub your feet and …."

"That sounds wonderful. Oh, I forgot your brother called collect." She tossed the next statement over her shoulder and continued out of the room. "He said he needs to speak with you."

Rahm watched his wife walk away with a hand to her back. She was tired. Chaz had already cautioned her that she might need bed rest for the last three months of her pregnancy, but she continued to push herself. He would do his best to convince her to take the time to rest.

He pulled his phone from his pocket. He hadn't spoken to his brother in a hot minute, mainly because he needed time to deal with everything that had transpired. *Might as well get it over with.*

Rahm dialed the private number that Daron had secured for him.

"Seals."

"Good …" Rahm checked his phone. "Morning. I need to get a call through to Cain Fosten," Rahm said to the warden.

"Inmates get their calls at night, not in the warden's office," the raspy voice on the other end responded, clearly irritated.

"Yes, sir, I'm aware. I remember from my time there, Warden Seals," Rahm stated, putting a watchful eye on his wife who was tipping back in with the last bowl of peach cobbler his Aunt Alyssa had made. She gave him a wink and a smile. *Oh, it's going to be a fight up in this camp.*

"Well, it's been a while, son. I'm glad you've kept your nose clean. I understand that you've done well for yourself."

"Yes, sir. I'm doing great," he answered, giving Marilyn a playful signal that he was going to spank her if she didn't leave him some. "Is it possible to speak with my brother for just five minutes?"

"You'll have to give me a few minutes," he responded. "It's a long way from his cell block to here."

Rahm's thoughts drifted while he waited. Of course, there would be no hold music played by the State Pen. No need to relax and get comfortable on that phone call, because it wouldn't last long enough. Besides, they didn't want anyone to feel that these kinds of things were anywhere close to normal. Rahm thought about the sequence of events that landed his brother in the Pen. Daron had showed him the footage and all he could say was he never believed his brother was stupid enough to not see that set-up a mile away. He had the real money, but his greed landed him with the counterfeit cash. Then to team up with his enemy? And what he did to their mother. Yes, his ass needed to be up under the jail.

"Why are you just calling me?" His brother's voice broke up his stroll down memory lane.

"What do you want, Cain? You're lucky I called you at all," Rahm said, sanitizing the tattoo bench while he talked. "It's more than you ever did for me."

"Please, can you put some money on my books? It's tough being in here without some cash."

He heard the weariness in his brother's voice, but it wasn't enough to break his arrogance. Cain still felt that everyone owed him something.

"How much?" he asked, giving Marilyn the evil eye because she was practically inhaling his peach cobbler.

"I need five hundred a month on my books. You can swing that since you riding with royalty and all that."

Rahm closed his eyes and listened to the warden tell his brother he had three minutes. "Why the hell did you go back to the house?"

"Man, I didn't steal anything from them. You would believe them over your brother."

Sitting on his bench, he allowed the quietness of the studio, and the feel of Marilyn's hand on his shoulder, to calm him. She had tipped back over the table where she left the bowl. *She thinks she's slick.*

"Yes, I believe them. One, they never lied to me or about me. Unlike you, who would do whatever you could to tarnish my name. Two, it's your greed that landed you in Menard in the first place. All you had to do was take that first money and be happy. It's that additional that got you in trouble. But even after you got that, you went to this man's house and stole money. I saw the video. They caught you on camera. Just why?"

"That dude didn't need that money," Cain yelled. "He had so much money in that safe; he'd never miss it. I wanted an opportunity to live a good life, as well. Is that too much to ask? Look, just put the money on my books."

"Yes, it was too much," Rahm protested. "These guys worked for every dime they have. You don't understand that concept. All you've ever understood is take, take, take and didn't even realize folks were giving. Well, maybe now you can learn what it means to work for what you receive. I will put some money on your books, but only one hundred dollars a month. You better take on some chores from the other inmates to earn whatever else you need. Have a great life inside, Bro."

Rahm disconnected the call before his brother could say anything else. He was going to have a hard set of lessons up in that camp.

He sat there for a few more minutes before he turned his focus to Marilyn. "Don't think I didn't see you polish off my peach cobbler."

"But what's yours is mine," she protested, batting her eyelashes trying to look all innocent.

"Yes, but that does not extend to peach cobbler. I will disown you when it comes to that wonderfulness that my aunt throws down."

"I saved you a bite," she said in a husky voice.

"It had better be more than a bite in that bowl or you're going to be in big trouble."

She lowered her gaze to below his waistband. "How much trouble we're talking?"

Rahm threw his head back and laughed.

# About the *Knights of the Castle* Series

Don't miss the hot new standalone series. The Kings of the Castle made them family, but the Knights will transform the world.

## Book 1 - King of Durabia – Naleighna Kai

No good deed goes unpunished, or that's how Ellena Kiley feels after she rescues a child and the former Crown Prince of Durabia offers to marry her.

Kamran learns of a nefarious plot to undermine his position with the Sheikh and jeopardize his ascent to the throne. He's unsure how Ellena, the fiery American seductress, fits into the plan but she's a secret weapon he's unwilling to relinquish.

Ellena is considered a sister by the Kings of the Castle and her connection to Kamran challenges her ideals, her freedoms, and her heart. Plus, loving him makes her a potential target for his enemies. When Ellena is kidnapped, Kamran is forced to bring in the Kings.

In the race against time to rescue his woman and defeat his enemies, the kingdom of Durabia will never be the same.

## Book 2 - Knight of Bronzeville – Naleighna Kai and Stephanie M. Freeman

Chaz Maharaj thought he could maintain the lie of a perfect marriage for his adoring fans … until he met Amanda.

The connection between them should have ended with that unconditional "hall pass" which led to one night of unbridled passion. But once would never satisfy his hunger for a woman who could never be his. When Amanda walked out of his life, it was supposed to be forever. Neither of them could have anticipated fate's plan.

Chaz wants to explore his feelings for Amanda, but Susan has other ideas. Prepared to fight for his budding romance and navigate a plot that's been laid to crush them, an unexpected twist threatens his love and her life.

When Amanda's past comes back to haunt them, Chaz enlists the Kings of the Castle to save his newfound love in a daring escape.

### Book 3 - Knight of South Holland – Karen D. Bradley

He's a brilliant inventor, but he'll decimate anyone who threatens his woman.

When the Kings of the Castle recommend Calvin Atwood, strategic defense inventor, to create a security shield for the kingdom of Durabia, it's the opportunity of a lifetime. The only problem—it's a two-year assignment and he promised his fiancée they would step away from their dangerous lifestyle and start a family.

Security specialist, Mia Jakob, adores Calvin with all her heart, but his last assignment put both of their lives at risk. She understands how important this new role is to the man she loves, but the thought that he may be avoiding commitment does cross her mind.

Calvin was sure he'd made the best decision for his and Mia's future, until enemies of the state target his invention and his woman. Set on a collision course with hidden foes, this Knight will need the help of the Kings to save both his Queen and the Kingdom of Durabia.

### Book 4 - Lady of Jeffrey Manor – J. S. Cole and Naleighna Kai

He's the kingdom's most eligible bachelor. She's a practical woman on temporary assignment.

When surgical nurse, Blair Swanson, departed the American Midwest for an assignment in the Kingdom of Durabia she had no intention of finding love.

As a member of the royal family, Crown Prince Hassan has a responsibility to the throne. A loveless, arranged marriage is his duty, but the courageous American nurse is his desire.

When a dark secret threatens everything Hassan holds dear, how will he fulfill his royal duty and save the lady who holds his heart?

## Book 5 - Knight of Grand Crossing – Hiram Shogun Harris, Naleighna Kai, and Anita L. Roseboro

Rahm did time for a crime he didn't commit. Now that he's free, taking care of the three women who supported him on a hellish journey is his priority, but old enemies are waiting in the shadows.

Rahm Fosten's dream life as a Knight of the Castle includes Marilyn Spears, who quiets the injustice of his rough past, but in his absence a new foe has infiltrated his family.

Marilyn Spears waited for many years to have someone like Rahm in her life. Now that he's home, an unexpected twist threatens to rip him away again. As much as she loves him, she's not willing to go where this new drama may lead.

Meanwhile, Rahm's gift to his Aunt Alyssa brings her to Durabia, where she catches the attention of wealthy surgeon, Ahmad Maharaj. Her attendance at a private Bliss event puts her under his watchful eye, but also in the crosshairs of the worst kind of enemy. Definitely the wrong timing for the rest of the challenges Rahm is facing.

While Rahm and Marilyn navigate their romance, a deadly threat has him and the Kings of the Castle primed to keep Marilyn, Alyssa, and his family from falling prey to an adversary out for bloody revenge.

## Book 6 - Knight of Paradise Island – J. L. Campbell

Someone is killing women and the villain's next target strikes too close to the Kingdom of Durabia.

Dorian "Ryan" Bostwick is a protector and he's one of the best in the business. When a King of the Castle assigns him to find his former lover, Aziza, he stumbles upon a deadly underworld operating close to the Durabian border.

Aziza Hampton had just rekindled her love affair with Ryan when a night out with friends ends in her kidnapping. Alone and scared, she must find a way to escape her captor and reunite with her lover.

In a race against time, Ryan and the Kings of the Castle follow ominous clues into the underbelly of a system designed to take advantage of the vulnerable. Failure isn't an option and Ryan will rain down hell on earth to save the woman of his heart.

## Book 7 - Knight of Irondale – J. L Woodson, Naleighna Kai, and Martha Kennerson

Neesha Carpenter is on the run from a stalker ex-boyfriend, so why are the police hot on her trail?

Neesha escaped the madness of her previous relationship only to discover the Chicago Police have named her the prime suspect in her ex's shooting. With her life spinning out of control, she turns to the one man who's the biggest threat to her heart—Christian Vidal, her high school sweetheart.

Christian has always been smitten with Neesha's strength, intelligence and beauty. He offers her safe haven in the kingdom of Durabia and will do whatever it takes to keep her safe, even enlisting the help of the Kings of the Castle.

Neesha and Christian's rekindled flame burns hotter even as her stay in the country places the royal family at odds with the American government.

As mounting evidence points to Neesha's guilt, Christian must ask the hard question ... is the woman he loves being framed or did she pull the trigger?

### Book 8 - Knight of Birmingham – Lori Hays and MarZe Scott

Single mothers who are eligible for release, have totally disappeared from the Alabama justice system.

Women's advocate, Meghan Turner, has uncovered a disturbing pattern and she's desperate for help. Then her worse nightmare becomes a horrific reality when her friend goes missing under the same mysterious circumstances.

Rory Tannous has spent his life helping society's most vulnerable. When he learns of Meghan's dilemma, he takes it personal. Rory has his own tragic past and he'll utilize every connection, even the King of the Castle, to help this intriguing woman find her friend and the other women.

As Rory and Meghan work together, the attraction grows and so does the danger. The stakes are high and they will have to risk their love and lives to defeat a powerful adversary.

### Book 9 - Knight of Penn Quarter – Terri Ann Johnson and Michele Sims

Following an undercover FBI sting operation that didn't go as planned, Agent Mateo Lopez is ready to put the government agency in his rearview mirror.

A confirmed workaholic, his career soared at the cost of his love life which had crashed and burned until mutual friends arranged a date with beautiful, sharp-witted, Rachel Jordan, a rising star at a children's social services agency.

Unlucky in love, Rachel has sworn off romantic relationships, but Mateo finds himself falling for her in more ways than one. When trouble brews in one of Rachel's cases, he does everything in his power to keep her safe—even if it means resorting to extreme measures.

Will the choices they make bring them closer together or cost them their lives?

## About the Kings of the Castle Series

*"Did you miss The Kings of the Castle? "They are so expertly crafted and flow so well between each of the books, it's hard to tell each is crafted by a different author. Very well done!"* - Lori H…, Amazon and Goodreads

Each King book 2-9 is a standalone, NO cliffhangers

**Book 1 – Kings of the Castle**, the introduction to the series and story of King of Wilmette (Vikkas Germaine)

*USA TODAY, New York Times,* and National Bestselling Authors work together to provide you with a world you'll never want to leave. The Castle.

Fate made them brothers, but protecting the Castle, each other, and the women they love, will make them Kings. Their combined efforts to find the current Castle members responsible for the attempt on their mentor's life, is the beginning of dangerous challenges that will alter the path of their lives forever.

These powerful men, unexpectedly brought together by their pasts and current circumstances, will become a force to be reckoned with.

### King of Chatham - Book 2 – London St. Charles

While Mariano "Reno" DeLuca uses his skills and resources to create safe havens for battered women, a surge in criminal activity within the Chatham area threatens the women's anonymity and security. When Zuri, an exotic Tanzanian Princess, arrives seeking refuge from an arranged marriage and its deadly consequences, Reno is now forced to relocate the women in the shelter, fend off unforeseen enemies of The Castle, and endeavor not to lose his heart to the mysterious woman.

### King of Evanston - Book 3 - J. L. Campbell

Raised as an immigrant, he knows the heartache of family separation firsthand. His personal goals and business ethics collide when a vulnerable woman stands to lose her baby in an underhanded and profitable scheme crafted by powerful, ruthless businessmen and politicians who have nefarious ties to The Castle. Shaz and the Kings of the Castle collaborate to uproot the dark forces intent on changing the balance of power within The Castle and destroying their mentor. National Bestselling Author, J.L. Campbell presents book 3 in the Kings of the Castle Series, featuring Shaz Bostwick.

**King of Devon - Book 4 - Naleighna Kai**

When a coma patient becomes pregnant, Jaidev Maharaj's medical facility comes under a government microscope and media scrutiny. In the midst of the investigation, he receives a mysterious call from someone in his past that demands that more of him than he's ever been willing to give and is made aware of a dark family secret that will destroy the people he loves most.

**King of Morgan Park - Book 5 - Karen D. Bradley**

Two things threaten to destroy several areas of Daron Kincaid's life—the tracking device he developed to locate victims of sex trafficking and an inherited membership in a mysterious outfit called The Castle. The new developments set the stage to dismantle the relationship with a woman who's been trained to make men weak or put them on the other side of the grave. The secrets Daron keeps from Cameron and his inner circle only complicates an already tumultuous situation caused by an FBI sting that brought down his former enemies. Can Daron take on his enemies, manage his secrets and loyalty to the Castle without permanently losing the woman he loves?

**King of South Shore - Book 6 - MarZe Scott**

Award-winning real estate developer, Kaleb Valentine, is known for turning failing communities into thriving havens in the Metro Detroit area. His plans to rebuild his hometown neighborhood are dereailed with one phone call that puts Kaleb deep in the middle of an intense criminal investigation led by a detective who has a personal vendetta. Now he will have to deal with the ghosts of his past before they kill him.

### King of Lincoln Park - Book 7 – Martha Kennerson

Grant Khambrel is a sexy, successful architect with big plans to expand his Texas Company. Unfortunately, a dark secret from his past could destroy it all unless he's willing to betray the man responsible for that success, and the woman who becomes the key to his salvation.

### King of Hyde Park - Book 8 -Lisa Dodson

Alejandro "Dro" Reyes has been a "fixer" for as long as he could remember, which makes owning a crisis management company focused on repairing professional reputations the perfect fit. The same could be said of Lola Samuels, who is only vaguely aware of his "true" talents and seems to be oblivious to the growing attraction between them. His company, Vantage Point, is in high demand and business in the Windy City is booming. Until a mysterious call following an attempt on his mentor's life forces him to drop everything and accept a fated position with The Castle. But there's a hidden agenda and unexpected enemy that Alejandro doesn't see coming who threatens his life, his woman, and his throne.

### King of Lawndale - Book 9 - Janice M. Allen

Dwayne Harper's passion is giving disadvantaged boys the tools to transform themselves into successful men. Unfortunately, the minute he steps up to take his place among the men he considers brothers, two things stand in his way: a political office that does not want the competition Dwayne's new education system will bring, and a well-connected former member of The Castle who will use everything in his power—even those who Dwayne mentors—to shut him down.

**Hiram Harris** is a premiere celebrity tattoo artist whose debut novel, Knight of Grand Crossing, which is being co-written with USA TODAY Bestselling author, Naleighna Kai, and National Bestselling author, Anita L. Roseboro, as part of the Knights of the Castle Series. Additionally, his character is currently featured in Kings of the Castle and King of Devon. The new series is being presented alongside his cousins, J. L. Woodson (Knight of Irondale) and J. S. Cole's (Lady of Jeffrey Manor).

www.hiramshogunharris.com

**Naleighna Kai** is the *USA TODAY, Essence®*, and national bestselling and award-winning author of several women›s fiction, contemporary fiction, Christian fiction, Romance, erotica, and science fiction novels that plumb the depth of unique relationships and women›s issues. She is also a contributor to a New York Times bestseller, one of AALBC›s 100 Top Authors, a member of CVS Hall of Fame, Mercedes Benz Mentor Award Nominee, and the E. Lynn Harris Author of Distinction.

She continues to "pay it forward" by organizing the annual Cavalcade of Authors which gives readers intimate access to the most accomplished writing talent today and the NK Tribe Called Success which offers aspiring and established authors assistance with ghostwriting, developmental editing, publishing, marketing, and other services to jump-start or enhance their writing careers.

www.naleighnakai.com

**Anita L. Roseboro-Wade,** a native of North Carolina is the only girl, and middle child of three children. Born to parents that never finished high school, this thereby fostered her drive and passion for the importance of education. She has a B.S. degree in MIS (Management Information Systems) and a Master's in Business Administration from Gardner-Webb University and the University of Phoenix respectively. Anita's passion for education is something that she has passed down to her sons. Instilling in them a deep-seated desire to achieve as much as they can while cultivating the gifts they were blessed to possess. Anita consistently strives to achieve excellence in every avenue of her life.

Now, as the road has finally curved to the path of her life-long dream of writing, she stands ready to take on the world as she lends her devotion and passion to her own life-long motivations. Anita is the author of Show Me No Mercy, a short story, Summer Breeze, and poetry in Heart Songs, a Poets and Writers Collective.

www.anitalroseboro.com

www.ingramcontent.com/pod-product-compliance
Lightning Source LLC
Chambersburg PA
CBHW011522240626
47154CB00009B/2933